Hosea's Heart

ENDORSEMENTS

Linda Rondeau's contemporary take on the Hosea story grips the heart, taking the reader deep into the lives of her characters. It's a page turner you won't be able to put down.
—Joy K. Massenburge, author of *A Cry for Independence*

Thought provoking presentation of forgiveness from different viewpoints. Ultimately, forgiveness of others is not likely unless we understand that we ourselves need the grace and mercy found in forgiveness. After more than thirty years in the mental health field, it becomes clearer and clearer that without the ability to forgive we cannot understand peace. This story demonstrates the complexity of both faithfulness and forgiveness. Unless we understand these concepts as recipients, we will not have the ability to extend them to others.
—Gina M. Reever, PhD, LCSW

Hosea's Heart is a compelling story of one man's commitment and his undying love for an unfaithful wife who repeatedly broke the marriage covenant. There are stories within the story filled with twists, intrigue, suspense and romance; yet each one bringing the reader back to the central theme of God's amazing grace and redeeming love.
—Rev. Norman Mesel, Lead Pastor of Turnpike Wesleyan Church

Hosea's Heart is a modern parable of God's unfailing redemptive power.
—Dalyn Woods, author of *My Sister's Keeper*

Once again author Linda Rondeau has given us a wonderful story, populated with characters to cheer on. This author has definitely established herself as force in the fiction realm. Readers will find their perceptions changed as they join characters who struggle with eternal truth and how to apply to life today.
—Edie Melson, award-winning author and blogger

Linda Rondeau's book, *Hosea's Heart*, is such a compelling and beautifully-told story that I read it in one sitting. I could not put it down.
—Sheri Dean Parmelee, Ph.D., member of ACFW

Hosea's Heart is an inspiring read, chock-full of intrigue and adventure, grace and mercy at every turn. As the story unfolds, you'll get caught up in this new suspense novel by Ms. Rondeau and race through the pages to find out how God takes what is unlovable and infuses hope into every situation. A read you will remember, and which could easily be my favorite of all her books.
—Jan Elder, Author of the *Moose Creek Series*

Linda Rondeau's latest novel grabs you from the beginning. This heart-breaking, redemptive story is a true winner. With Rondeau's talented art in describing the scenes, bringing to life the characters, and capturing the thread of spirituality woven throughout. From the beginning where a modern day version of the Biblical Hosea's love for a wife that strays from her vows of marriage through the scenes that bring an unexpected but satisfying and truly epic ending, Rondeau keeps us panting for more. I heartily recommend this book.
—Carol Brown, author

When a husband's dreams are shattered by his wife's desertion, he opens his heart to give hope to a city's underworld. When she returns, he has a choice to make. This contemporary story inspired by ancient events reveals how God's mercy transcends the pain of desertion and deceit. Mrs. Rondeau's story of a modern-day Hosea provides a poignant example of loving forgiveness.
—Johnnie Alexander, author

A love story that pulls at your heartstrings and takes you on an emotional roller coaster ride with twists and turns that will keep you turning the pages.
—Michele Chynoweth, Author of *The Faithful One, The Peace Maker* and *The Runaway Prophet*

What readers are saying about Linda Wood Rondeau

I love how Linda Wood Rondeau's stories flow so smoothly and that her characters are believable.
—JoAnn Stewart, reader

Reading Linda Wood Rondeau's books is like wrapping yourself in your favorite blanket and going on a journey that is much anticipated
—Maria Bourgeois, reader.

For a satisfying read, Linda Wood Rondeau delivers original plots, complex characters, and real life situations that mirror her years as a social worker.
—Cleo Lampos, author

Linda Wood Rondeau's books will grab your heart and not let go.
—Carol McLain, author

Sparks meets Sue Grafton. The twists and turns keep readers intrigued and soon readers are rooting for the protagonist to succeed against all odds.
—Gregg Golson, reader

What I love about Linda Wood Rondeau's books: well-developed, ordinary, relatable characters and the sprinkling of humor throughout her books. I love her way with words.
—Cass Wessel, reader

I am yet to read a book by Linda Wood Rondeau that doesn't contain 3D characters that linger long after the last page is turned.
—Clare Revell, author

Linda Wood Rondeau has a way of putting the reader into the characters' heads. The reader feels invested in the story.
—Jacqueline Kimball, author

I am a big fan of Linda Wood Rondeau's books. They always have story lines and wonderful characters that keep me reading.
—Ann Lacy Ellison, reader

Typical review comments

—words that draw you in like the smell of cider on a chilly afternoon. Lovely.

—She keeps you turning pages with her wit, descriptions, humor, and great writing.

—the author has a way with words that is unique and brings to life a story that touches the heart.

—-an AMAZING talent & her books NEVER disappoint

—stories that are hard to put down.

—great warmth and humanity with surprising depth.

—this author's writing delivers: suspense, humor and good writing. Books that stick with you!

Hosea's Heart

Linda Wood Rondeau

Contemporary Fiction

Elk Lake
PUBLISHING, INC.
PLYMOUTH, MASSACHUSETTS

Cover and Interior Design: Derinda Babcock
Editor(s): Cristel Phelps, Deb Haggerty
Published in Association with the Seymour Agency

PUBLISHED BY: Elk Lake Publishing, Inc., 35 Dogwood Dr., Plymouth, MA 02360, 2018

Library Cataloging Data
Names: Rondeau, Linda Wood (Linda Wood Rondeau)
Hosea's Heart / Linda Wood Rondeau
184 p. 23cm × 15cm (9in × 6 in.)

Description: **How much should a wronged husband forgive?**
This time, Aubrey Beaumont's wife has left for good. Though a single dad with three children to raise, Aubrey diligently searches for his drug-addicted, runaway wife. Fifteen years later, he has relocated from Vermont to Silver Spring where he serves as a respected minister and chaplain. He is caught in a quandary when he is called to a community hospital to counsel a terminally ill patient and comes face-to-face with his long-lost wife.

Identifiers: ISBN-13: 978-1-946638-94-6 (trade) | 978-1-946638-95-3 (POD) | 978-1-946638-96-0 (e-book.)

Key Words: Love, Marriage, Infidelity, Forgiveness, Family, Contemporary Romance, Gangs
LCCN: 201894921 / Fiction

DEDICATION

No one can truly comprehend the hell of addiction without witnessing its grip … either through personal experience or losing a loved one to its power. This book is dedicated to those struggling with Addiction's hold. May you discover through this work, the One who loves you most.

ACKNOWLEDGMENTS

No book comes together without the help of many dedicated helpers. This list is in no way conclusive. First of all, thank you readers. Without you, I'd have no reason to write. You are the thought and life behind the words God gives me. Thank you to Julie Gwinn, The Seymour Agency, and to my editors, Cristel Phelps and Deb Haggerty. Thank you, Elk Publishing, for believing in this work. Most of all, thank you to my patient and encouraging spouse of nearly forty years and to my children who have always encouraged me not only with words but with their example. Thank you family and friends for listening to my groans, my fears, and reminding me God is in control.

PROLOGUE

Aubrey Beaumont's heart pounded as Darlene burst past stodgy Mrs. Donovan and ran into his arms. The girl's reddened eyes confirmed his worst fears.

"Mommy went away again, Aubrey."

Darlene sobbed against his overcoat while he absorbed the news. From the entryway, he saw Paul and Bradley at the kitchen table, frozen to their seats, remnants of peanut butter sandwiches on their plates. Paul guzzled the last of his milk, and Bradley rocked back and forth as he hummed "Jesus Loves Me."

"Thank you for staying with the children, Mrs. Donovan. I rushed out as soon as the seminary gave me your message. I don't suppose you know where Joanna went off to, do you?"

She handed him a note tucked inside Joanna's wedding ring.

"Sorry, Mr. Beaumont. I got here my usual time, and your wife handed me this package like it were a present. Then she stormed out the door. Slammed it so hard, she done bust the hinge. Said I was to stay here with Darlene and the boys 'til you came home. Then she slapped a twenty-dollar bill in my hand. 'For the inconvenience,' she said. 'Taint no inconvenience. I love these kids as if they were my own."

Aubrey gripped the parchment paper—Joanna's curt goodbye. She'd never left a note before. Usually, she slithered away during the night. This time she left while the sun still shone. He slid the gold-edged stationery from its circular perch as he gazed toward Mrs. Donovan. "Did my wife say anything else?"

Mrs. Donavan lumbered toward the coat rack. "Nope. Just high-tailed it out that door." She twirled as she wriggled her wide body into a coat three sizes too small. "Didn't even take her purse. Walked out with just the clothes she wore … no coat or nothing." She grabbed the doorknob with one hand and snatched her straw purse off the counter with the other. "Look, I gotta get home to my Artie. I fed the kids. Want me to come back after I take care of that rascal man of mine and put them to bed for ya?"

Sorrow would have to wait.

"You've done more than enough already. I'm sorry my wife caused you trouble. How can I make it up to you?"

"Ain't no bother." Mrs. Donovan stroked Darlene's cheek. "Not when it comes to these here precious ones. Don't worry none about your seminary studies, either, Mr. Beaumont. I'll look after the children for as long as you need me to."

Aubrey shoved the ring and note into his pocket. "I appreciate your kindness. I know my wife's behavior has made it difficult for you at times."

Mrs. Donovan crossed her arms. "Maybe a tad. But I figure, if I help you reach your ministry goals, it'll be like I've done my own mission work."

Aubrey gifted Mrs. Donovan a kiss on the cheek, as a son to a mother. "You tell Artie he's one lucky man."

Her ruddy complexion deepened to a crimson red. "How you talk, Mr. Beaumont. I'll be here when the rooster crows to get the kids off to school." She covered his hand in a maternal clasp. "Personal feelings aside, I do pray Mrs. Beaumont comes back. She always has before."

"I don't know. Something in my gut tells me this time is different."

She arched her back and huffed her condemnation. "Any woman can walk away from these sweet ones don't deserve 'em. That's all I got to say." With that, she headed out the door and scooted to the green clapboard house next door.

He gasped—a protracted breath, a prelude to an expected dawn, though he never wished for this day to come.

Fischer had predicted this end when asked to be Aubrey's best man. "She's gonna break your heart. Mark my words, buddy." His "I told you so" wafted on the air, though the man nowhere in sight. Aubrey chewed his lower lip and sighed. He'd grieve the end of his marriage later. First, the children.

He unglued Darlene from his coat. "Time for bed, guys."

"Can't we wrestle first, Daddy?" Paul asked.

Darlene gazed toward the cluttered table. "Kitchen needs to be cleaned up." She grabbed a towel and went to work. He thought how matronly she'd become, this daughter not of his blood but of his heart. As if to fill a mother's void, she read to the boys, certain to tell Aubrey whenever they needed discipline. Her azure eyes gazed up at him. "I won't cry anymore, Aubrey. I know Mommy's not coming back this time." She tapped her chest. "I feel it inside."

Paul and Bradley slipped from their chairs, and Aubrey tackled them, the green-shag carpet a mat of delight as he diverted his tears to momentary laughter. Paul squeezed free like a greased pig at the fair. He laughed like one too.

A sudden pain shot across Aubrey's shoulder, a signal the game needed to end for tonight. "Go to your room, guys. I'll be in for prayers in a bit." The twinge grew into raging pain. What happened to that burly quarterback from Brattleboro High? He'd have to accept the fact he could no more prevent the advancement of years than he could keep his runaway wife at home. Time moved forward with or without her.

He hobbled into his sons' bedroom, instantly enveloped in memory. Joanna had redecorated their room last summer, right after her third rehab. She'd searched every department store in town before choosing the sport-themed decorations. "Boys need heroes, Aubrey," she'd said as she carefully hung posters of the legends: Babe Ruth, Ben Hogan, Bobby Orr, Wilt Chamberlain, and Johnny Unitas. Aubrey's favorites, too, and evidence of a love she could never verbally express.

Bradley sat on the lower bunk, his head cocked like a question mark. "Daddy, I know I should pray for Mommy to come home. I don't want her to. She's mean to Paul. I don't think she loves us boys very much. She loves Darlene, though." He dove underneath the covers, turned his body around, and fell into a fetal position, cocooned within his comforter.

"You're wrong, son. Your mother loves both of you."

Paul hauled himself up to the top bunk and stared at the ceiling. "Sometimes, I feel a little love inside the slap."

"Mommy doesn't slap me," Bradley said, "because I'm invisible."

Aubrey stood at the door in momentary silence. He should argue his sons' assessments. Why butt his head against the truth? Still, maybe someday they'd understand how the drug stole their mother's goodness.

What minimal words could he offer to reassure these tender hearts? "Try not to be mad at your mother. She needs our prayers even when she's not with us."

"If you think we should pray for her, then I will," Bradley said.

Paul closed his eyes and pretended to be asleep.

Delayed grief demanded expression—tears too strong to hold at bay now flowed. Aubrey hugged his boys, grateful they still needed him. Soon, they'd shy away from even manly embraces.

"Good night, guys." He closed the door on their simpler world where hugs and wrestling matches made a motherless life tolerable.

He returned to the kitchen. The scent of Joanna's afternoon cinnamon tea assaulted him as he picked up her favorite white mug from the table. Aubrey took the dishcloth from Darlene's hands. "You've done a wonderful job in here, Sis. It's time for bed. I'll finish up for you."

"I did my best, Aubrey. That's what you always told us. Do your best, no matter how much it hurts inside." She shuffled toward her bedroom.

His tossed-back words hit like a hard-driven pitch as he ambled toward the living room and sunk into a recliner. He closed his eyes in memory of happier days—their one-week courtship and hasty marriage. Would he marry her again if he knew how the romance would end?

A moot question. Life rarely offered mulligans.

Darlene's soft shuffle dissipated his musings. "Did I interrupt your rest, Aubrey?"

He smiled. "No. Don't ever be afraid to talk to me—anytime—at rest or not. Okay?"

"Okay. I'm ready for bed now."

Her long tresses set off high cheekbones fortressed by a determined jaw, the image of her mother. Darlene kissed him on the cheek. "Good night, Aubrey. Don't worry. The boys and me—we'll be okay because we have you." With that, the woman-child strode to her room.

He pulled out Joanna's farewell from his pocket and gazed at her last sentiment to him. *Don't try to find me. Take care of Darlene.*

From habit, Aubrey reached for his Bible—his constant companion. Within its pages, he found wisdom, direction, and strength. He chortled at the irony. Joanna, who challenged his faith at every opportunity, had been the catalyst that propelled him into ministry. Her words uttered in ridicule had struck a God-given chord. "You spend so much time in that Bible, Aubrey, you should be a minister."

Regardless of how he came to this path, he never doubted God's call. If only Joanna would believe. Though he'd led many to a life of faith, his wife repeatedly rebuked the God he loved.

Joanna's most recent rehab had been court-ordered in lieu of incarceration. "Your last chance," the judge said. Perhaps the last chance as far as man's judgment was concerned. Aubrey had wrapped Joanna in his arms. "God will help you beat this, my love."

She had shoved him away. "You're wrong, Aubrey. If God exists, he wants nothing to do with me."

Sudden rage filled him. Not toward Joanna, though often he wished he could despise her. Why couldn't he rescue the one person who meant more to him than any other? He rubbed the gold band on his finger. "Don't you know I'd have given my life for you?"

This inescapable truth renewed him. If she were to walk into the room, even now, he'd welcome her back as he had countless times before—his need for her as addictive as any drug.

He'd find her, no matter how long it took.

CHAPTER 1

FIFTEEN YEARS LATER

The Reverend Aubrey Beaumont stepped from the elevator onto the hospital's third floor and halted like a sniffing bloodhound.

Cinnamon!

Since he'd become a chaplain for Mercy Hospital, cinnamon greeted him far too often. He blamed Rita Harrington, the head nurse. She probably sensed his aversion and drank the flavored beverage purposely to goad him. He determined not to become fodder for her twisted pranks.

His stomach moaned.

Cinnamon tea—Joanna's favorite.

Fifteen years since she left him, and still the aroma accosted his memories. He despised this weakness. Like Superman's kryptonite, cinnamon challenged his manhood. His face was probably pallid by now. Should he leave before Rita noticed? Better she thought him irresponsible than a wimp.

Too late to turn around. She hollered to him from the break room. "I'll be right out, Reverend. Keep your collar on!"

Except when dry heaves threatened his masculinity, Rita's insensitive jokes failed to rile him. He normally took three deep breaths when agitated. Not possible now without inhaling the cinnamon. Escape from the aroma would be his only salvation. "No need to hurry, Rita. Enjoy your break. I'll check on Percy and talk with you later." He readied to leave at a dignified clip.

"Wait a minute, Reverend. I've some news about Percy. I'll be out in a second."

From where he stood, he could see her tap the cinnamon stick against the rim of her cup before she tossed the offensive spice into the wire wastebasket. If possible, the air intensified with the loathsome scent, and nausea threatened his forced composure.

Rita emerged and repositioned her stethoscope. "Percy's being discharged tomorrow. Thought you should know."

"I hoped he might be."

"Quite the recovery he's made. All I can say is you must have a lot of influence with the Almighty. When he came to us, he was so thin his ribs stuck out like a poster child for a relief mission. His social worker said they found his cupboards stocked with food. Interesting how Alzheimer's patients can have all the food in the world to eat but can't remember to fix their supper."

He resisted her bait. No need to engage in senseless banter about the evils of a mind-crippling disease. All too often, Rita's casts had more to do with gossip than a patient's care or to impart her vast knowledge. She could pry open the most closeted of secrets from a CIA agent.

When Aubrey didn't respond, she changed tactics. "Of course, sudden onset of depression in the elderly is a common occurrence," she added with encyclopedic authority.

His only escape would be his duty. "Anyone else I should see while I'm here?"

"Don't think so. Fairly quiet the past few days. If we need another miracle, you'll be the first to know. By the way, Percy's been moved to Transitions, Room 404—last room on the left."

Aubrey entered the archway dividing the long-term care section from the medical floor. Far from Rita's station, the horrid scent of cinnamon oddly intensified the closer he came to Percy's room.

Was he hallucinating? Percy didn't drink tea. The odor jerked at his memory like a fishing line. Why did this cinnamon encounter unnerve him more than most? Then, he realized. Today would have been his twenty-fifth wedding anniversary. A reason to celebrate if he knew his wife's whereabouts.

He glanced at the room across the hall, his curiosity drawn to the door left ajar, yet guarded by two police offers. Was an inmate in that room?

He knocked on Percy's door, then entered. He sat in a bedside chair, his ear two inches from the television. A Golf Channel biographer spewed amazing facts about the legendary Bobby Jones. How should he grab Percy's attention? A shout loud enough to be heard over the television might very well bring down Rita Harrington's wrath.

Aubrey waved a hand in front of Percy's face.

He turned. "Oh! Hello, Reverend." Though emaciated beyond description, his grip proved to be twice as strong as a man's half his age "I hoped you'd be by. Gettin' out of here tomorrow."

"That's what Nurse Harrington says. Where are you going?"

Percy cupped his right ear in his palm and leaned forward. "Heh?"

This time Aubrey shouted loud enough to be charged with disturbing the peace. "Where are you going tomorrow?" So much for confidentiality.

Thankfully, Percy hit the mute button. "Discharged to my daughter's care. She's gonna stay with me until my house gets sold. Then, I guess I gotta go into a nursing home."

How Gregg Fischer could find Percy's daughter with so little information, yet give up on Joanna, boggled the mind. "When did your daughter arrive?"

"Day before yesterday."

Most considered Aubrey a sentimentalist, a trait Joanna had often ridiculed. This occasion warranted a hallelujah regardless of one's stoicism. He and Fischer had orchestrated this magnanimous reunion, a highlight usually reserved for talk show hosts. With God's help, they'd made an old man's wishes come true. "I'm happy for you, Percy."

"Don't act like it was nothin'. Don't know how you and your friend found her. I couldn't so much as remember my phone number when I came in here. Matter of fact, can't recall much of the last forty years."

Percy unmuted the television. How could a boring clergyman compete with golf history? Aubrey searched for a clue to leave or stay—some recognition from the patient his minister was still in the room. Percy jolted as if sudden memory pricked him. He turned off the television. "Where are my manners? Please, sit a spell."

Aubrey sat in a bedside chair.

"Don't know how you convinced my Cindy to come all the way from Chicago to see me after all these years. Poor girl musta hated me for sure, the way I just took up and left her and her mother."

To say Percy's smile stretched from ear-to-ear was no exaggeration, his face so shrunken, a smirk would spread from cheek-to-cheek. "Say, did ya know she's a school teacher? Imagine that. Percy Logan, high school dropout and a scoundrel of the worst order—the father of a teacher. Ya know what else?" He motioned Aubrey to lean in for the secret. "She's right handy on the golf course too. Club champion ten years in a row."

"Don't say?"

Tears streaked Percy's cheeks. "Don't know how I got so duped, thinkin' my family wuz better off without me. Don't remember why I took off like I did. I was drunk and stayed that way for the next twenty years. By the time I sobered up, I wuz half a country away and too ashamed to come back."

Aubrey smiled. "Glad you realized it's never too late to seek forgiveness. Where there's breath—there's hope."

Percy clasped his hands together. "Sure hope so, Reverend. Cindy said her mother forgave me afore she died. Gettin' to know my Cindy again is more than a fool like me deserves."

Life had taught Aubrey many things, including the fact God's grace extended to drunken fathers and wandering wives as much as the faithful. "I'm glad the two of you found each other again."

"God's doin' for sure. Shame all those years got tossed away like yesterday's newspaper. Hoping I can make up for lost time." Percy swiped his eyes with a wrinkled hankie.

"Will I see you at church?"

Percy picked up his Bible and stroked its leather cover, like a woman's hand on mink. "Cindy promised she'd bring me. Doc says I can't drive no more."

"I'll keep an eye out for you."

Percy glanced toward the television. "Got a lot of talented players these days, but I don't think there'll ever be another Bobby Jones. Retired too young, if you ask me. Amazed he never went pro."

Aubrey watched the segment on Golf's Greatest Legend. Jones was a lawyer by occupation, yet his contribution to a great sport would never be equaled. Would Paul reach such great heights? Only a year since he went pro, but who was to say? Maybe in time, he'd see Paul play in a major tournament. A father should be able to dream for his son, shouldn't he?

Aubrey thought of the Master's hand on Percy's life, honored to lead the contrite oldster in a sinner's prayer. His instantaneous reformation amazed even the skeptical Rita Harrington. And now, God had granted Percy reconciliation with his child.

If only the Lord would do the same for Joanna.

How was it Fischer could fill a dossier on a drunk's daughter whose last known address was forty years old but couldn't locate the only child of a congressman? The unarguable reason—Joanna didn't want to be found. Perhaps the time had come to give up the search.

Percy rose with difficulty and plopped on his bed while the television remained at full volume. "Guess it's my nap time." He leaned back and scanned Aubrey's full height. "Ever played basketball, Reverend? A tall feller like you has got to be a man of sports. Lean too. I expect you're pretty light on your feet."

"I played basketball in college, though I excelled more in football. Played quarterback in high school. Unfortunately, UVM didn't have a football program when I attended."

"UVM?"

"University of Vermont."

"What's the M stand for?"

"The name comes from the Latin meaning University of the Green Mountains."

"That explains it. Can't expect no Latin-named school to excel at sports. Now, French is another story. Just look at Notre Dame."

"You'd be surprised, Percy. UVM is up and coming in the sports world."

Aubrey stooped so Percy's neck wouldn't strain as he peered into his pastor's eyes. "You know, Reverend. I'm ashamed of the things I done, ashamed I never tried to find my wife and daughter. Yet, I never stopped lovin' my sweet little girl."

"Dad, I'm forty-five, hardly a little girl anymore."

Though they'd never met in person, after twenty phone conversations, Aubrey would have recognized Cynthia Prescott's midwestern accent anywhere. She leaned against the doorframe. "You must be Aubrey Beaumont."

"How did you know?"

"Your voice sounded familiar, and the clerical collar is a giveaway, although I thought they'd gone out with the reformation."

Obsolete for some, perhaps. "I wear it as a reminder of why I went into the ministry. It's a long story. I won't bore you with it."

Her laugh teased him like a musical interlude on a happy flute.

"I enjoy long stories. Perhaps you'll enlighten me at dinner Sunday? I want to repay you in some way for your kindness to my father."

"Nice of you to offer." His face heated while he stared. Hypnotic green eyes called him back to the pine-encapsulated hills of his youth.

CHAPTER 2

Joanna heaved a sigh of hope. "Glad you realized it's never too late to seek forgiveness." The minister had said the words yesterday to the old codger across the hall. The visitor had to shout to be heard, perhaps God's megaphone to her. Though she couldn't see his face, his voice cracked her memory, as resonant as fifteen years ago—Aubrey. If so, did he mean what he'd said? Could she finally find his forgiveness?

She'd never know unless she tried.

What about the red-headed woman who went into the old man's room shortly after Aubrey? She'd visited several times over the last few days. Though Joanna hadn't seen the woman with Aubrey before, she seemed to recognize him.

Joanna eyed the clock—church would be ending soon. Should she send for him? If she did, would he even come? She'd have to manage the request through Rita Harrington, who made no pretense to hide her animosity toward her criminal patient. Rita would not surrender information unless she herself would benefit.

Joanna had believed Aubrey gave up his search after she last saw him while he handed out pamphlets to prostitutes. A few quick questions to Joey's pimps confirmed the man who masqueraded as Reverend Hank was indeed Aubrey. She'd learned he had moved from Brattleboro to Silver Spring where he pastored a church. How foolish to flaunt his religion in front of Joey Juarez, one of the cruelest drug czars in Washington's underworld. One who'd never tolerate any mission work in his territory. Joanna had called Gregg Fischer and told him to warn Aubrey ... to tell him that, in all probability, his wife was dead, to give up the search and move on.

Aubrey didn't move on. If Gregg had warned Aubrey, the words had fallen on deaf ears. He continued his work on Eastern Ave week after week, a man obsessed. For his sake, she'd kept their past connection from Joey, and convinced him the minister's efforts would have little to no impact on Joey's cartel. "Besides, Reverend Hank's antics might prove to be a source of amusement." That alone satisfied Joey ... at least until last month. Who knew what he might do without Joanna there to dissuade him? Things were different now. Perhaps the Lord had paved a way for her to finally approach the only man she'd ever truly loved.

Joanna pressed the call button.

Rita burst into the room, a mixed air of affected coyness and theatrical annoyance. "You know, we're short-staffed today. I hope you called me in here for a good reason."

Better to ignore the barb than get sucked into a discussion about Rita's hectic work life. Pleasantries were wasted on a woman like her. Joanna dove in. "Do you have a chaplain here?"

"Reverend Beaumont is one of our chaplains. Father O'Brien, the Catholic priest, is the other."

"Will Reverend Beaumont be in today?"

Rita fiddled with her stethoscope. Next, she'd probably pick up a glass or find something to straighten. The woman busied herself as purposelessly as a gerbil on a wheel. "Normally, the chaplains visit only as requested on the weekends. Reverend Beaumont is on call for today. He'll need a reason. What should I tell him?"

Although a competent nurse, Rita required a greater motivation than the ilk of human kindness to move outside her job description. "I have personal reasons."

Rita's glare shook Joanna's resolve. Perhaps she should call Gregg Fischer and threaten doom if he didn't convince Aubrey to go back to Brattleboro and forget his marriage … be free to love again … maybe the red-headed woman.

Rita oozed a contentious breath. "You do know he has church duties in addition to those as chaplain. He's very busy."

"I'm aware his time is valuable. Do you know Reverend Beaumont? Personally, I mean."

Rita fluffed her patient's bed pillows. "He's a good friend."

Joanna squelched her cynicism. Doubtful Aubrey would choose a friendship with someone like Rita Harrington. Nor was it likely she attended Aubrey's church. "Out of curiosity, is Reverend Beaumont married?"

Not that she would blame Aubrey if he'd divorced her and found someone else. Sometimes Joanna prayed that he would do just that. He had legal grounds—even Biblical ones.

Rita lingered. She picked up dirty linen and tossed trash into receptacles as if desperate for the next gossip morsel. "I assume he's married, though I never asked him directly. He wears a wedding ring. Why do you ask?"

Then he did find someone else. The red-headed woman?

"I think a married man would be better able to help me." She hesitated, fearful to bring back memories of happier times. "Does he have children?"

Rita opened the blinds, a sadistic move since she knew bright sunlight hurt her patient's eyes. "You shouldn't wallow in the dark." Finally, she turned to answer the dangled question. "I believe he has three children. A daughter, Darlene, recently finished law school and works in a prestigious DC firm."

Oh, if I could only see her … let her know how proud I am of her.

As Joanna hoped, Rita spewed like a volcano. Like most gossipmongers, intimate details flowed regardless of veracity. Joanna cupped her hands to still the tremors, afraid to know the answer, yet she must. "And the other two?"

Rita put her hands on her hips. "Do you need a chaplain or are you hiring him to pastor your church?"

I've come this far … I won't stop now. Joanna grabbed the Lord's lifeline in the form of an agitated nurse. "I'd feel more comfortable if I knew he understood children."

Rita snickered. "Why? How many do you have?"

A fountain ceases to flow without a source. Rita wanted information of equal value, details beyond common knowledge to her colleagues. The Maryland Attorney General's office had insisted on Joanna's anonymity. Only her doctor, who had been carefully vetted, knew his patient's identity. The AG had also insisted that she be cared for only by charge nurses who would manage her chart under the alias of Jacey. Rita was not the only administrative personnel who found the order a major inconvenience, beneath her station to empty bed pans and sweep the floor.

Perhaps if Rita's mysterious and troublesome patient provided some nugget of insight into her importance, her nurse would give Joanna what she most desired … to see Aubrey one more time before the Lord took her home.

"I also have three children, though I haven't seen them in a long time." Would that be enough for the gluttonous Rita Harrington?

"Reverend Beaumont seems equally proud of his boys. The youngest, Bradley, is a graduate student at the University of Maryland, College Park. He's going to be a counselor, so I hear. Guess he takes after his dad."

Better his dad than his mother.

"And then there's Paul."

Joanna's jaw clenched. "Is something wrong with Paul?"

"Not at all. He's a professional golfer on the European Tour. Most broadcasters predict he'll join the PGA in a year or two and move stateside."

Aubrey … you've done a marvelous job without me. Perhaps better than if we'd stayed together.

Rita stood by the door, hands crossed over her chest. "Anything else you need to know?"

Joanna rose from her bedside chair, though her legs threatened to buckle. Her care plan stipulated she was to get out of bed only with assistance. Rita made no move to help her patient. Once steady, Joanna sat on the newly made bed. "No. Thank you, Rita. I'd appreciate a call to Reverend Beaumont. It's important."

As expected, Rita readied to play her trump card as she stood in fossilized impatience. She'd spewed—now she expected information in return before she'd grant a favor. "Your chart says you're not to have visitors." By now, she'd gleaned enough information to talk the ear off anyone who cared. Apparently, she wasn't satisfied.

How much more could be shared with her nurse? If she were to see Aubrey, Joanna had no other recourse than to give Rita her prize. "Lucas Skylar has granted permission for clergy visits. You can ask him yourself, if you'd like."

A great deal of information, indeed. Not even the hospital administrator knew that the AG's office had been responsible for the cloistered medical services to a terminally ill patient. Rita's wide grin showed stained, large front teeth. "I'll call Reverend Beaumont right away. I understand you're being transferred tomorrow to a hospice center?"

Joanna hesitated. Did Rita want to know which one? If more were divulged, Lucas might take the plea agreement off the table, though Joanna hadn't yet agreed to testify. His constant badgering perhaps more from their long-ago relationship. What right did a college romance give him to pester her now? "Thanks again, Rita. Would you please make certain the door's ajar when you leave? I despise closed places."

No surprise—Rita slammed the door shut.

Joanna lacked the strength to walk to a chair let alone across the room to open a door. Her chest constricted. She grabbed the oxygen mask. Such an ugly thing, and the weight against her sallow cheeks, another source of discomfort. What a dilemma. When she'd come to the hospital, she prayed for a quick death. Now she prayed for extra time, time enough perhaps to witness God's hand in these her final days.

The door creaked open, and Officer Casey, her angel in blue who knew her aversion to closed doors, gifted her with a compassionate smile.

While her breathing returned to quasi-normal and her chest relaxed, her thoughts drifted back to Aubrey. What if he refused to see her? He'd have no way to know he'd been summoned by his runaway wife. If Rita failed to clue Aubrey on Joanna's transfer, since the request was not an emergency, he could postpone the visit a day or two.

Once more she asked God to orchestrate the improbable.

CHAPTER 3

Week after week, he prayed for a dose of old-fashioned, get-all-excited-about-it, Holy-Spirit visitation. However, today's service fit the on-going, disappointing norm—albeit some blessings—a good attendance, a great blend of worship music, and a special by the Kelsey twins. The service followed the bulletin down to the scripted congregational prayer—yet all transpired within an unenthusiastic atmosphere.

What did he expect? Their pastor was not a great orator by any shape of the imagination. The board had asked him to present more energetic sermons and to order services that might appeal to younger families. What? He should dance? He preferred a more straightforward, three-point delivery backed up by Scripture.

He discovered long ago his ministerial gifts did not include public speaking. The larger the attendance, the more he stammered. Why did God call him to preach when he lacked charisma? He cared deeply for his flock, though his motivation for coming to Silver Spring had been in a hopeless pursuit to find Joanna after Fischer had made some off-beat remark he thought he'd seen an arrest warrant for a Joanna Curtis on one of his internet searches.

Public speaking had always caused Aubrey to stammer. Even Joanna wondered why he chose the ministry. "Ants like sugar, Aubrey. You give the people vinegar."

After yet another failed sermon, he looked forward to a pleasant afternoon at Percy's home. Though he initially hesitated at Cynthia's invitation to dinner, he was glad he accepted. As he rummaged through the parsonage's oak cupboards for something to contribute, he hummed "The Jericho Road," an old hymn he'd heard his grandfather sing. He tapped his foot in rhythm to the upbeat melody. He closed the last cupboard door. Absolutely nothing suitable.

A homeless man would starve in Aubrey's kitchen. He kept little in the pantry since the children left home and preferred to eat out. Parishioners' dinner invitations brought respite from the tasteless food at Luigi's Diner—although lately, invites had become as infrequent as a warm day in January.

Or perhaps, there was a deeper reason than diversion for this elevated sense of wellbeing. Cynthia raised a hope in him he thought dead. For the first time in fifteen years, he fantasized the possibility of a romantic relationship. He must bring something. Candy? Flowers? Wouldn't the gesture be premature when the invitation suggested nothing more than a simple expression of appreciation for kindness rendered in the line of duty?

He'd fought the idea with disciplined repression—yet, Cynthia's emerald eyes invaded his sleep. In the dream, he was a boy again, hiking up Mt. Olga. As he neared the peak, the dream changed. She waited at the top. As he neared the summit, Joanna's voice called to him. "Don't abandon me, Aubrey. I need you."

When he awoke from the dream, his course seemed as uncertain as the day before. Why pursue a hope obviously lost? Fischer lectured that Aubrey deserved some happiness this side of Heaven. "Move, on Beaumont," he preached, his advice laced with far more passion than Aubrey's Sunday sermons.

For all he knew, he was a widower by now. Mortality rates were high for heroin addicts. Why not ask Cynthia out? She was as beautiful as she was intelligent, and the combination invigorated him like a brisk walk at sunrise.

The shrill ring of the landline prompted him to seek immediate relief. For once, his private thoughts had amused him, and he disliked the interruption. Would the world end if Aubrey Beaumont let the landline ring until the answering machine picked up? If it were important, they'd call his cell next.

No. He must not let a call go unanswered. He was God's servant, always available, not merely at his convenience. "Silver Spring Community Church. Pastor Aubrey here."

"It's Rita Harrington."

The last person he hoped would call. Better to listen to Deacon Yates's critical review of today's sermon than be dressed down by the formidable Rita Harrington.

"There's a woman at the hospital who wants to speak with you. She says it's urgent, though I don't know what she thinks constitutes an emergency."

Aubrey took a minute to process this dilemma. To cancel his dinner invitation seemed unforgivable. "I have immediate plans. I could be there later this afternoon. Maybe she'd rather speak with Devon O'Brien? He might be able to get there sooner. He owes me a favor or two."

A perturbed grunt and then, "I'm pretty sure she wanted to speak only with you. I'll ask if she can wait until you can be here."

Aubrey looked at his watch while canned music vibrated in his ear. He'd be late. Though Cynthia might forgive his tardiness, he would not forgive himself. Punctuality was his middle name. He glanced at his watch a second time. What was taking Rita so long? He'd asked a simple question requiring a yes or a no. After five minutes, Rita's voice replaced the theme from Titanic.

"She says she'd rather speak with you. She'll wait until you get here. No matter how late."

"I'm assuming she's a patient and not a visitor."

"Yes. Admitted last week."

She'd been there a week? Odd he should be called only now. "Why haven't I seen her? I've been in twice since then."

"Her circumstances are unusual. She's under guard."

The patient across from Percy?

"Is she violent?" He rebuked his fear. A man of the cloth should be available to anyone regardless of criminal record.

"No. Not in here anyway."

"What does that mean?"

"Of course, I found this out on the Q-T, but I happen to know she's a material witness in a big state case. My guess it's the Juarez trial."

Great. Would he be on Juarez's hit list if he spoke to this patient? "I'm familiar with the name."

Rita harrumphed. "What do you know about the likes of Joey Juarez? Doesn't the good book say light should have no business with darkness?"

Big mistake. He should have pled ignorance. He'd been careful to keep his street ministry a secret, especially from the church elders. No one at the hospital need know their chaplain masqueraded as Reverend Hank in the middle of Juarez territory. The normally careful Reverend Beaumont had let down his guard, and Rita zoomed in like radar. "Hasn't Joey Juarez been all over the news lately?"

"Yes, of course. A headliner for the past two weeks."

Aubrey blew out relief. He'd dodged another Harrington bullet. "If your patient's problems are drug-related, why is she at Mercy?"

"We've stabilized her medically. She's being transferred tomorrow."

Rita baited his curiosity—only this hook might prove to be deadly. "I suppose I should know what her diagnosis is if I'm going to counsel her."

"End stage pulmonary carcinoma. Based on her symptomology, I expect she only has weeks to live."

No wonder she wants to see a clergyman. "How old is she?"

"I'd guess mid-forties. She has no family—at least none I know about."

"Am I allowed? I'm assuming visitors are closely monitored."

"She has permission for clergy consultation. The patient asked for you specifically."

He pulled out a pad from his jacket pocket. "What's her name?"

"She's kind of a mystery patient. No one knows her real name. Her chart says Jacey."

Aubrey jotted down the scant information. If nothing else, the visit should prove far from routine. "Thanks, Rita. I'll be there at four."

Aubrey dialed Cynthia's number. If it were anyone else, his curiosity would have demanded he cancel his dinner engagement. Cynthia Prescott was not anyone else.

CHAPTER 4

Cynthia disconnected the landline. *As courteous as he is handsome.* She shouted into the living room. "Reverend Beaumont's on his way, Dad."

He winked. "You know, Cindy, he's available. Sort of."

Just what she needed. A romance with a sort of available guy. "This dinner is merely a thank you. I'm not looking for anything more."

"I might be ancient, but I still know when a man has a twinkle in his eye. He looked at you like I looked at your mother first time I seen her."

"Dad, you're exaggerating."

"Not a bit. I say reel him in, little girl. A catch like that don't swim by every day."

"I'm not in a fishing frame of mind." A romantic interlude? Preposterous and ill-timed. Reacquainting with a father she barely knew took all her emotional energy right now. Besides, being single didn't mean the end of the world. Cynthia silently counted her failed romances after Donald died. One disaster after another. Each hopeful relationship blew up before the fourth date. Frank only wanted her bank account. John dumped her for her best friend. She broke up with Dave after he crashed his motorcycle and truck in the same week.

She'd wearied of the chase. If God wanted her to remarry, he'd have to hit her over the head with the evidence. She shrugged her shoulders. Useless to think of a special relationship with Dad's minister. Besides, he had a wife—somewhere.

Aubrey thrust the bouquet at his hostess, and Cynthia sniffed the flowers. "Thank you, Reverend Beaumont. Mums are my favorite. How did you know?"

Not an original thought, yet true. "Lucky guess." Her smile lit the room. She deserved a finer array, better than a last-minute purchase at the convenience store when he stopped for gas.

"Please, call me Aubrey. Reverend sounds stuffy."

"I just assumed, given you still wear a clerical collar, you'd prefer the title."

"Easy enough assumption to make. Most everyone calls me Aubrey or Pastor Aubrey except the older parishioners and Rita Harrington."

The so-called hard of hearing Percy chuckled from the living room. "Yep. Rita Harrington is apt to be the only nurse in Silver Spring still starches her uniforms. Maybe what makes her so uppity."

Aubrey caught Cynthia's strained smile. "Excuse me, Reverend … er … Pastor Aubrey … while I put these in water. Feel free to join Dad in the other room. He's watching ESPN."

He felt like a kid who had to decide between ice-cream or cookies. As much as he enjoyed a sports show, he wanted to be near Cynthia. "Need help?"

Her eyes danced like those of an Irish goddess. "Not unless you know how to mash potatoes?"

"Matter of fact, I do."

"Follow me."

He scanned the old house. The darkened white cupboards bore the smudges of neglect despite the hint of lemon and ammonia scrubs. With a little work, however, the house could be restored to its original lavish design. The mahogany woodwork and decorative plaster ceilings dated the home to the late 1800s. "Love this old house. Architecture is a hobby of mine."

Cynthia handed him a potato masher from the island drawer. "Mine too. It's going to take a while before I get this place presentable for the market. I've taken an indefinite leave of absence to tend to Dad's needs."

Selfishly, he hoped she'd stay in Silver Spring for a long time. However, the counselor in him took center stage. Was she overreacting because of sentimentality? Too often he'd seen parishioners reorder their lives on a whim only to regret their decisions later.

He drained the potatoes, and the rising mist enhanced the scent of her perfume. He stepped back as Joanna's face clouded before him then disappeared when the mist dissipated.

Best to engage in small talk. "Your father must be pleased you've decided to stay."

"I'm not sure he grasps what I'm doing here. I'm glad he knows who I am, though."

"I have found in these situations that the caregiver needs personal outlets. Do you have any other interests besides teaching, Mrs. Prescott?"

She glared. "If I am to call you Aubrey, it's only fair you call me Cynthia."

"Very well … Cynthia … what do you like to do in your spare time? Your father told me you're an excellent golfer."

"I don't know about that, but I would like to try out the local links. Winter here is much milder than in Chicago, though I am used to cold-weather golf."

He shouldn't let on what he already knew. "What's your handicap?"

"You mean besides my swing? I play scratch mostly. At least I used to. I haven't played as much since my husband died."

She brushed near him to reach a pot holder, and his face heated. He poured the milk and added butter then beat the potatoes with sufficient vigor to match his arousal. When his heart rate slowed, he tapped the masher against the side of the pan. "No lumps."

Cynthia leaned over to examine his work. Why did his attraction to her prompt guilt?

"Perfect. Thanks for the help." She retrieved a large glass bowl from the pantry and handed it to him. He took the hint and spooned the potatoes into the dish. "Dad apparently didn't spend much money on dishware. Besides the chipped plates, all I could find were a few bowls and one meat platter."

"It's not the plate that matters but what's on it."

"A man's point of view, I suspect. Everything's ready. I hope you like Cornish hens?"

Truthfully, the tiny, lean poultry made him think of Gulliver's Lilliputians. "I eat anything."

Pleasant aromas of a home-cooked meal filled his senses—the meal surprisingly delicious. Or perhaps the company enhanced his appetite. He'd always found conversation to be an excellent condiment. However, in Cynthia's company, more like an aphrodisiac, though they discussed nothing paramount, like war or politics. Aubrey excelled in small talk, probably because he preferred to listen before he added a sentence or two of his peculiar expertise. Conversation opened the window of the heart—what occupied the mind most reflected the quality of a soul.

Cynthia's laughter soothed like an expensive balm. More than wit and charm, tantalizing enough, she wooed him with those Erin-go-bragh eyes. His joy in her company unsettled him. When near her, he acted the klutz. Fischer would tell him to forget Joanna—to seize this amazing opportunity.

As a counselor, Aubrey often told his clients to turn over the abandoned partner to God's care, to move on and accept the good God offered.

Those clients were unbelievers whose marriages were legally dead, perhaps by virtue of a former partner's remarriage. Since Aubrey was a Christian when he married Joanna, he held himself to a different standard, though no one would blame him if he gave up the search. He wearied of a life in limbo, married yet not married.

Some days he wished he could accept an opportunity to know love again, to hold a woman in his arms, to taste the nectar of hungry lips. Joanna was a ghost—yet, an ever-present aura. Cynthia was no apparition—rather flesh and blood—and he sensed her attraction to him as well.

Aubrey glanced at his watch, more out of habit than a need to know the hour. Seemed an appointment of some kind always loomed only minutes ahead. If he were to be at the hospital on time, he'd have to leave in the next few minutes. How could he tear himself away from so enjoyable an afternoon? Would the Universe shatter if he were a few minutes late?

"I'm sorry to rush off. I have an appointment. Thanks again for dinner. Maybe we can mash potatoes together again sometime?"

"Yes. Perhaps we can." Cynthia took his extended hand into hers and smiled. Her lips, thickened by a hint of strawberry lipstick, innocently invited a kiss. He summoned the strength to stand back. If he were to kiss her, he'd want to possess her. Was he truly free to do so?

CHAPTER 5

Gregg Fischer grabbed his Red Sox cap, scooped up the keys to his Porsche, hummed a few bars of "Georgie Girl," and headed toward the door. As his cell chimed "Take Me Out to the Ball Game," he considered if he should answer.

The call might provide him with an excuse. He'd run out of reasons why he never went to Jason's hockey games. A father should be more attentive. Since Marla died, his son lived apart from a father. Why should he change the status quo?

Gregg pulled the cell from his pocket and checked the incoming number. "Hello, Beaumont, you scamp! Haven't heard from you in over a week."

"I've been busy. How's everything in Brattleboro?"

"You know how it is. Nothing ever happens in Vermont."

"Got a minute?"

Gregg sprawled onto the couch and threw his keys on the coffee table. "For you, old friend, I've got all day. What's up?"

"Do you think it's too late for an old shoe like me to start dating again?"

"I'd say not. Best hurry, though. Your sole's about worn through."

Gregg felt a ping in his conscience. He'd managed to keep Joanna's secret for two years. Better Beaumont believe her dead as she requested. He'd wasted half a lifetime on that conniving broad, fixated on the notion Joanna would return to her childhood roots.

"Who's the lucky girl?"

"Cynthia Prescott."

Gregg whistled. "Don't blame you. From her pictures, I can tell she's a looker."

"Beautiful doesn't begin to describe her. It's the whole package, Fischer."

"It would have to be for you, you old stuffed shirt." Even in his wildest days, Beaumont treated women as treasures, not conquests, and his gallantry attracted coeds like children to the Pied Piper.

"I can't ask her out yet. I'm still married."

Beaumont would die the most old-fashioned man on the planet. "You're only married in your mind because of some silly piece of paper.

You don't know who Joanna might have shacked up with since she left you. You have enough to get a divorce if you want one. Do you?"

"Maybe it's time to grasp reality."

Cynthia Prescott must be an amazing woman to turn Beaumont's head one-hundred and eighty degrees. "Exactly what I've been telling you for the last fifteen years."

"Fischer, do you think Joanna left me because I failed her as a husband?"

"No one can shoulder the happiness or discontent of another. Something I shouldn't have to tell you. You're the counselor."

"I really hoped we'd find her with the last lead. Maybe God moved me here for another reason."

"I told you a few years ago, I thought I saw her in DC. Apparently, I mistook someone else for her."

Sometimes, friendship required a lie, didn't it?

"You did your best to find her."

With Beaumont's renewed interest in the dating world, Gregg huffed with a sense of exoneration. *I did the right thing for once in my life.* He'd keep Beaumont in the dark for as long as necessary. Maybe one day the truth would out. By then, perhaps he'd be remarried and happy for once in his life.

Besides, if Joanna wasn't dead already, how long could anyone expect a heroin addict to survive?

"You have to face the truth. Joanna is never coming back. You've waited more than any other man would have."

"Not knowing hurts more than knowing. Fischer, I loved her with my whole heart and soul. I think I still do. The idea of starting over seems silly to me now. Not when I'm still in love with Joanna."

"You're only in love with the memory of her, Beaumont. Let go. She made your life a veritable hell on earth. Or have you forgotten?"

Amazing how dead silence often screams pain.

Faint breathing followed—Beaumont would change gears. "So, any word from Briggs Detective Agency?"

He should have called before now, the reason for hesitancy a mystery to himself. Since childhood, the two men shared their news like an old married couple—each calling the other over weather reports and baseball stats.

"I got the call Friday. I'll be moving to DC in a week. Long as you're on the phone, can I crash with you until I find my own place?"

"I'll have to clear it with the elders, though, I don't foresee a problem. It'll be great. I've missed our Monday Night Football sessions."

"What's that ding?"

"The elevator. Gotta go, pal. Duty calls. Talk to you later."

"I'll text my flight plans as soon as I make them." Gregg disconnected. If he were a praying man, he'd have shouted a "hallelujah" that Beaumont finally saw the light. Though they spoke frequently, perhaps a move to the DC area would help best buds revisit those boyhood days in Brattleboro. Great times—especially the Friday night movies at the Latchis Hotel. Not all friendships endured time as theirs had. Perhaps years wiped away the foolish prattle of childhood taunts. He could only recall one true argument between them, when Beaumont announced his intention to marry Joanna Curtis.

He hadn't said a prayer since Marla died. Maybe he should start again. Satisfied his non-planning always worked magic, he picked up his keys, tossed them into the air, caught them on the descent, and headed out the door to catch the last period of Jason's game.

CHAPTER 6

Aubrey pocketed his cell as he exited the elevator onto the medical floor.

Rita hovered nearby. Wasn't she supposed to go off duty by three? "Punctual as usual, Reverend Beaumont." She smiled or smirked, one could never tell. "Jacey's expecting you."

A heavy-set police officer stood in sentinel fashion outside the woman's door. Aubrey stopped before he reached her room. Common sense told him to run, to let Devon O'Brien handle this one. Curiosity proved more potent than reason.

He addressed the guard as he approached the door, left slightly ajar. "I'm Reverend Beaumont, here to see the patient in this room the nurses call Jacey."

"You may go in, Reverend Beaumont."

As he entered, his knees weakened with the onslaught of the scent. Cinnamon tea! His eyes moistened as he stood frozen in time and place. He should be filled with joy. Yet, sorrow permeated the flood of emotions at the sight of her. Though a skeleton of her former self, she still resembled a portrait with all the allure of a Mona Lisa. When he last saw her, golden curls fell over her shoulders. Instead, dark tresses, threaded by strands of salt and pepper, now wrapped her slender shoulders.

He thought her a hallucination at first. She appeared an image much like the time he first saw her—vulnerable and in need. The alias should have warned him. Fischer thought perhaps she'd reverted to her maiden name after she left.

She cocked her head, and a seductive smile stretched across her face. "Hello, Aubrey. Happy anniversary, darling."

CHAPTER 7

Joanna blinked with the awkwardness. His shock must be more than surprise. Disgust? He stood before her like a statue, stiff and immobile. How awful she must look to him—a breathing corpse.

"Lost for words again, I see. Come now. Can't you say hello? Try it. Your jaw is already dropped. Say the first syllable, close your mouth, and the rest will follow. Hello." She exaggerated the facial movement for his benefit. "See how easy it is?"

"Is it really you, Joanna?"

Aubrey never could string an original sentence together. Ironic how his worst quality allured him to her, a Moses in need of an Aaron.

"Yes, Aubrey." She swung her feet to the side of the bed and waited until the pain ebbed enough for her to stand. "Forgive me if I'm not as spry as I used to be. It takes me a minute or two to move from one place to another."

Predictably, Aubrey rushed to her aid, and she, of course, refused. And predictably, he sighed with frustration. Still the protector with an outstretched hand to stay the inevitable tide—a Don Quixote who charged the windmills. She stopped, unable to take another step, grateful for Aubrey's help to the bedside chair.

As she sat, he stepped back. "I don't know what to say. I thought I'd never see you again."

"Because you thought I died? Or maybe you only hoped I had?"

"I always hoped I'd find you."

She clenched her teeth to deny pain a victory. "Not like this, I imagine." Acidity coated her words—sarcasm too natural an outlet, a habit she'd relied upon to stave off true emotion. Would she slash Aubrey's manhood as she'd done a thousand times before? She hadn't meant to wound. She only wanted to tell him how deeply she regretted the wasted years. Yet, within the first few minutes of their reunion, she'd cut him again.

Where to begin? She only knew how to spew venom. Could she share an honest thought? So much God could teach her about life, if only she had more time. The adage true—too late wise.

Rita Harrington burst through the door. "Sorry for the interruption. Time for your medication." After she confirmed her patient's date of birth for the gazillionth time, Joanna swallowed her pills while Rita glared at Aubrey. "Do you two know each other? From before, I mean?"

Joanna looked at Aubrey and shook her head. Would he heed the warning? Keep their relationship a secret? For Aubrey's sake, Joey must never know their connection.

Gentility won over common sense. "You might say we know each other. Joanna is my wife."

"Oh!" Rita hesitated a polite ten seconds before she galloped out of the room, probably to alert her favorite tabloids—anonymously, of course, to save her job. At least, there'd be no more interruptions while she fueled the media train.

Joanna stared with wonder at the man who'd so bravely aligned himself with her. He knew the risk. Perhaps she shouldn't have asked to see him. Better he believed her dead. She would be soon enough.

Nevertheless, he came as she'd hoped. She must tell him. No small talk. No more slicing at the wind. Truth sometimes hurt more than lies and would require her to reward faithfulness with additional pain. "I suppose you want to know why I've suddenly decided to show myself."

He sat on the bed like a child who waited for his favorite bedtime story, his cheeks moistened by escaped tears.

Aubrey's faith, always so strong, might give him the power to forgive so much wrong against him. Could she expect the same from the children? Had they found independent faith? Or did their religiosity remain under their father's shadow? She could only expect their rejection. Still, they deserved to know the truth.

Aubrey held her hand. "Are you a witness or something against Joey Juarez?"

To answer would put Aubrey's life in danger.

"I know all about Juarez."

She studied his face. No. He didn't know everything. Despite his street ministry, Aubrey was still a man child, incapable of complete comprehension of evil. Joey stained the sidewalks of Eastern Avenue with more blood than any of his competition. Shame filled her. Drugs had brought her so low, she'd bedded with Satan's brother.

"How much did Rita tell you?"

"Not much. I put the pieces together as far as Juarez is concerned. She told me about your cancer, and that you're being transferred to a hospice care facility in the morning."

How much more should she share? Aubrey deserved to know the full extent of her predicament. "Lucas Skyler has agreed to provide medical care outside of prison if I plead guilty to prostitution and agree to be a witness against Joey. I pled out to the lesser charge, but I haven't made up my mind to testify."

"Lucas Skylar is with the Maryland State Attorney's office, isn't he?"

Aubrey wore fear like an overcoat. She remembered how his cheeks drew inward when confronted with the horrific. "You seem troubled. St. Mary's is a wonderful place. I'll get the best of care."

"I thought perhaps that's where you'd be sent."

"You're worried because—?"

"I don't think you'll be safe there. It's not as secure as the hospital."

"Safe from what? Joey won't bother me."

"Are you sure?"

"Pretty sure."

How surreal to talk with him in this way. Not the conversation she imagined. "I need to ask you something. Has Gregg Fischer said anything about me recently?"

Aubrey paled. "Fischer? He thought you might be in the DC area. That's why I moved here. Earlier today, he said he thought he'd been mistaken."

Exactly what she hoped he would have said. "I saw him at a subway stop near Union Station a few years ago while he was visiting you. I assumed he might tell you where I was. At the time, I'd already undergone several rounds of chemo. We chatted for a bit, and I told him I didn't expect to live very long. He doesn't know I'm currently in the hospital or if I'm still alive—for the time being."

"Fischer knew and didn't tell me? Why?"

"Don't be too hard on him, Aubrey. Our meeting at Union Station was not an accident. I found him after Joey told me about a nosy private detective he wanted to rub out. When he described the man, I knew Joey had meant Gregg. I told Joey I'd get the guy off my tail. I warned Gregg not to tell you anything about me, Joey, or the cancer."

"I would have found you. Given you the best medical care ... I know a lot of doctors."

"I've been given excellent care, Aubrey. Most people don't live this long with stage four lung cancer. I also saw you a few times on the street corners while you did your masquerade as Reverend Hank. Though mostly amused, Joey worried you might upset his territory. I convinced him you wouldn't save enough people to make a difference and that he might as well ignore you."

Aubrey snickered. "Thanks for the confidence."

"Not what I meant."

"I know. I guess I should be grateful you kept Juarez from killing me. Unfortunately, you're right. Very few of the girls came to me for help. Mostly, they saw me as a free grocery store."

Joanna smiled. Aubrey's kindness still knew no limit. "That was the talk on the street."

"Fischer should have told me regardless of your wishes to the contrary."

"He never liked me and believed your ignorance was in your best interest. The one thing we agreed on."

She gasped for breath and coughed uncontrollably. She prayed she would not lose consciousness. Should she ring for Rita to put her back to bed?

Aubrey handed her a glass of water. She took small sips, and the coughing subsided. "There's so much to say and so little time."

He gazed at her as if pensive. "I've always said the best place to start is at the beginning. I'm not going anywhere."

The words cleansed her soul, though no doubt served to pierce Aubrey's. Yet, he must know everything. She held nothing back, not even her unholy union with Joey and the high-priced international escort service she ran.

His face twitched as she confessed. Halfway through her torrid revelation, he veered his glance toward the window.

"As you can see, Aubrey. God's punishment is just."

He walked to the other side of the room. "It has been worse for you than I ever imagined." He pulled over a chair, sat, and put his arm around her shoulders. "I would have given my life to spare you from this end."

"I know."

"I won't lie to you. I'm troubled, of course, but I do want to understand. Go on. Please."

The medication took affect and her body numbed. Blessed sleep would soon take over. "I won't be awake much longer, Aubrey. This medicine is not enough to kill the pain. Only enough to take the edge off so I can sleep for a few hours."

"Can't they give you anything stronger?"

"I refused opiates. I will not go out addicted. My treatment is more palliative than curative, though Lucas wants me to try an experimental drug. He thinks if he prolongs my life, he'll eventually persuade me to testify against Joey."

Aubrey leaned back. He stroked her hand. "Do you need to rest?"

"Not yet." There was so much more to tell him. How could she relate the horror she experienced as Joey's mistress—the final beating that led to spiritual submission? The Aubrey she remembered abhorred violence and refused to allow a gun in the home. "I think my coming to faith was a gradual awakening, like coming out of a deep sleep. Criminals like me know they walk the line between life and death. Since you and I met, I wanted to change—to be the person I'd been before I started using— someone of quality. After so many failures, I gave up the fight, convinced myself death would be my only escape. I actually prayed for the end."

Aubrey turned away. She imagined his thoughts. How many times had he told her that God's forgiveness was only a prayer away? Instead of owning grace, she pleaded for death.

"Apparently, though I gave up on God, he did not give up on me."

He faced her. "What are you saying? Are you a Christian now?"

She expected his disbelief. "Yes. I am."

"When? How?"

"About six months ago, Joey beat me for the hundredth time ... the worst I'd experienced. I was sure I would die. I don't know how long I lay there drenched in my own blood before I found enough strength to crawl. I must've knocked over my purse during my struggle with Joey. Lipstick, tissues, and a comb were strewn across the floor. Odd. Almost as if they'd been strategically placed. There next to me, I saw the only picture I'd kept from our marriage—the one taken at the Topnotch during our short honeymoon at Stowe."

"You've kept it all this time?"

"Guess I wanted to remember a time when I'd been happy. We did have a few good years, didn't we?"

He nodded. "I remember Stowe as if it were yesterday. We watched the sunset from the fireplace. I thought there could be no more beautiful place on Earth. I really thought we were going to make it."

"I did, too, even though I carried another man's child."

He didn't need to ask the question. She saw the pain in his eyes. "If love could have cured me, I'd still be with you, Aubrey. I tried. I so desperately wanted to be clean—for your sake. And the children. Self-determination is a poor substitute for God's grace."

He held her hand in his. "And you've accepted that grace?"

"As fresh blood seeped from my mouth, I expected death would come in minutes. If I were going to die, I figured I should at least go out with a whimper of remorse. I didn't ask God to spare me, instead I recited a litany of my sins. More than an account of wrongs, I discovered a sincerity of regret that I'd spurned the one hope I knew. Was I too late? Suddenly, I wanted to live. Besides forgiveness, I asked God for hope, a little more time—to find some purpose in all I endured. With my last bit of strength, I called 911."

Aubrey's eyes narrowed. She didn't blame his disbelief. "And have you found a purpose?"

"While in the hospital, I received a visit from a domestic violence worker. Rather than condemn me, she listened. I remembered how you described salvation, God's unconditional love. As I gained in physical strength, God gave me courage. I turned myself in to Lucas Skylar. In exchange for a guilty plea, he arranged for house arrest and hospice care. My medical needs have exceeded the limits of home care. Lucas believes St. Mary's is the right place for me. Near enough for him to badger me to testify."

She shivered.

"Are you cold?"

"I'm always cold. Nature of the beast, I'm afraid."

Aubrey grabbed the extra blanket and wrapped it around her. "I hate to ask the question."

"Ask."

"How long? Do they know?"

"A month, maybe two."

"There's nothing more the doctors can do for you? Surgery? Clinical trials?"

"No. The cancer's spread to the liver and the bones. Thankfully, not the brain."

He held her hands. "We'll make the most of what time we have. One never knows. The Joanna I remember would fight for every breath."

She expected him to be civil—thoughtfully curious. The depths to which he still loved surprised her, and tears of remorse spilled, though she'd been determined to hold them back. He'd suffered so much all these years. Pain she inflicted on him. Now she'd hurt him again.

"Lucas wants to get me into a drug-trial program. What's the point?"

"Skylar doesn't own you."

Yes, he does, Aubrey. More than you know. "Not strictly speaking."

Aubrey closed his eyes as if in prayer. "Joanna, God is gracious maybe—"

"Don't, Aubrey. Complete remission is not God's plan for me. He kept me alive long enough to save me. There's grace in that, isn't there?"

"Yes, of course. I can't bear the thought of losing you again so soon."

A radial pain shot through her chest.

"Is there anything I can do to make you more comfortable?"

"The pain comes and goes." She sighed, not from pain but from guilt. "I have told you everything I can. I didn't ask you to come here to be my nurse. I only ask for your forgiveness. And to set you free."

"I don't want a divorce, Joanna. Especially not now. May I visit you again, at St. Mary's?"

More than she'd hoped for. "I'd like that."

Aubrey squeezed Joanna's hand, then walked from the room. He went to the restroom, grateful to be alone with his shock, too numb to sense grief. Thankfully, Rita was nowhere around.

He entered the elevator engulfed in an emotional fog. Where should he go? What course would God require of him? He'd hoped for this day since she left. Now, he stood mute, helpless, confused.

She'd asked for his forgiveness. He hadn't said the words. Could he truly give her what she wanted? Did he still love her, or had he only hitched his love to a memory like Fischer said? Perhaps the Joanna he once loved died, a specter within the frame of this woman who vaguely resembled his wife. He'd believed himself to be a man of character, a man who could forgive any wrong perpetrated against him—until she dashed his self-delusion with her confession. He'd heard worse from inmates who bared their sins without compunction. Those were confessions with six degrees of separation from the hearer—unknown wounded souls—detached from his heart. Their stories unfolded like a B-rated movie.

He'd forgiven her drug use before she abandoned him for the last time. However, her liaison with Juarez was a cake of bitter herbs, a betrayal far worse than heroin.

Green eyes and soft features framed by red hair crept across his mind. What about Cynthia? Only a few hours before, he entertained the thought of a romance. Aubrey glanced at the plain gold band he'd worn for twenty-five years. For better or worse, he'd promised before God and men. Cynthia deserved a man who would be free to love her openly, someone who could give her a future. Aubrey Beaumont could not be that man.

Something else nagged him like an unreachable itch. How could his best friend have deceived him for so long? A true friend would have defied Joanna and told the truth.

He parked in front of the church. Funny. At Tuesday's board meeting, he mourned the need for a locked church. He believed God's house should be a sanctuary for the needy, not a social club for believers. Why couldn't they find a way to patrol the church so that the building could remain open when those in darkness most needed respite?

Fortunately, in his dark hour, he had a key.

Each step resounded against the marble floor as he walked past the offices to the chapel alcove used for small group prayer. During the week, he, as well as two assistant pastors and a full-time secretary, bustled about the building. Most requests came from nice people whose faith had been strained over car repairs and appendectomies.

Silver Spring Community Church nestled between two residential developments—a sea of multi-level homes with three-car garages, in-ground swimming pools, and the acquisition of the latest technological advancement. He loved his flock—yet sometimes, he was angered over his sheep's self-centeredness. The street ministry, though he remained incognito, or so he thought, gained the greatest portion of his missionary heart—the place he believed he accomplished the most.

Had he fooled himself into the belief God needed him? Had he entered the ministry out of pride? Did he seek out the lost for their benefit or for his own self-esteem? Was his zeal a mere delusion? If so, he'd been the worst of hypocrites. One who admonished others to love the unlovely, yet stood unable to offer complete forgiveness to his own wife. Why couldn't he utter the words Joanna wanted to hear?

Did he hold back because God succeeded where Aubrey had failed?

The magnitude of his sin weakened him—his failure to trust God with Joanna's spirit. He'd pursued her like a lost dream as if he alone held the key to her redemption. He should have known. One can only lead a soul where God has already begun the work. Until now, he counted his good deeds like the entrepreneur totals his revenues. How foolish. The lost did not need his platitudes.

True, he risked his life on many occasions to bring baubles of hope to outcasts whose midnight shadows blackened the graffiti-adorned avenues. And he prided himself on his bravery. He read a few Bible verses, handed out tracts, and offered fewer prayers. On one occasion, he slipped a hundred dollars into a hooker's purse and told her to go home.

A foolish act. While he prided himself on his generosity, the poor girl probably used the money to buy more drugs. Emptied of their glamor, his humanitarian efforts now seemed paltry. He spent his hour on the street then returned to the squeaky-clean floors and lemon-polished furniture in his parsonage.

Perhaps God sent Joanna back to him, not to serve his manly needs, but rather to show him his starved spiritual condition. He ran his index finger along the mahogany altar rail, the last remnant from the old sanctuary. The congregants desired a flashier setup and tore down the centuries old edifice. At Aubrey's request, the elders placed the antique altar in the small alcove chapel, out of sight but still useful. When he prayed here, he imagined the saints of yesteryear who wept in contrition, each stain an emblem of a spiritual battle fought and won.

"Oh, God!" Aubrey knelt to meet the mauve carpet while his tears of remorse mingled with those from the past. "My sins are great. For these I ask forgiveness. Now I ask for strength to do what is right."

The hours immeasurably passed while he knelt in conviction. He whose life revolved around clocks and watches basked in a Holy Presence and let time drift.

CHAPTER 8

Aubrey stared at his cell. Should he call the children? Joanna didn't ask nor did Aubrey offer. Yet, a preemptive contact on Joanna's behalf seemed prudent. He prayed God would soften their hearts.

He'd call Darlene first—Joanna's child, whom Aubrey adopted while still in the womb, his name on her birth certificate the only one of record. He'd watched her soft heart harden, like scar tissue over a wound. Rather than confront her resentment, she'd fought her anger with accomplishment. She'd sailed through undergraduate school. Her yearbook caption read like a Who's Who entry—drama, literary club, debate team, yearbook staff, basketball, soccer, and dean's list all four years. She graduated with highest honors although law school proved to be more of a challenge. Her inclusion into the prestigious law firm of Preston & Harrowitz had been well deserved.

Though he prided himself in Darlene's achievements, he feared for her soul. She heaped activity upon activity and filled her waking minutes with projects, challenges, and self-imposed deadlines—contentment, like the rabbit's carrot, never within reach.

Aubrey called his children every Wednesday, the best time to fit fifteen minutes into everyone's complicated schedule. He hit Darlene's number from his speed dial directory.

She sounded out of breath as she answered, "Aubrey? Did the world come to an end? It's Sunday, not Wednesday."

How to begin? "I intended to start with small talk. No way to subtly begin, I'm afraid."

"You always told me to blurt a thing out and sort through it later."

"Okay, then. Here goes." He sighed. "We've found your mother."

Complete silence.

He waited a few more seconds. "Sis? Did you hear me? We found your mother."

"Alive or dead?"

Whether desired or not, Darlene inherited her mother's sarcasm.

"She's alive. I can't tell you anything more for safety reasons."

Hesitation. Then, "What does that mean?"

"I'll explain later. Darlene, she's changed."

A snort. "Are you sure? What does she want?"

"Nothing."

"Why has she decided to be found, now, after all this time?"

How much to reveal? "She doesn't know I'm calling you and your brothers. Nor did she ask me to. Something else you should know. She's a Christian."

"Is that supposed to erase all those years? If it makes her happy, fine. Her new beliefs won't change my feelings one iota. I wouldn't be surprised if she pretended to have found religion to get her hooks into you again. Who knows what her real agenda might be. She was always manipulative."

"True enough in the past. Your mother is a very sick woman and wants to die in peace. If you want to see her. I'll arrange it."

"I've nothing to say to her. She's a stranger to me."

"I think you should."

Silence. "What about Paul and Bradley? Are they going to see her?"

"I haven't told them yet. I called you first."

"You know we never bought into your 'she's sick' explanations when we were kids."

"Regardless. You're all grownups now, and she needs our support."

"If our seeing her means that much to you, fine. Make the arrangements. I'm busy this week. I could probably squeeze a visit in before the end of the month. Gotta go. It's late and I need to get to work early tomorrow. Bye, Aubrey."

She disconnected before he could reciprocate her farewell.

Paul spoke through a yawn. "Dad? What's up? It's not Wednesday. You do know it's only four in the morning here."

"Sorry I woke you." How easily one forgot the varying time zones.

"I'm up by five most mornings anyway. I like to hit the practice links early. So why did you call? Something wrong?"

"Nothing's wrong. I have news."

"If it's about Bradley, I already know. Don't worry. I wouldn't miss my little brother's wedding for all the championships in the world."

Bradley's getting married? Better to be last on the notification list than not on it at all. Neither Bradley nor Paul offered much information without a cattle prod. They talked to each other at least. "It's not about Bradley. And what's this about a wedding?"

Paul laughed, although Aubrey saw nothing funny concerning his patriarchal ignorance.

"Sorry, Dad. Guess I let the cat out of the bag. I'm sure he meant to tell you on Wednesday. The wedding's not until Christmas."

"Not until? You do realize Christmas is only six weeks away. I'm sure he'll let me know when he gets around to it—sometime before the wedding would be nice. I'd like an invitation at least."

Paul's contagious chuckles billowed through Aubrey's sorrow. "Don't worry. I'm sure he'll call soon. He and Trish wanted to keep the ceremony a small affair. Invitations will be by word of mouth or sent via social media."

He cringed. "Bradley's wedding. He should do things his way."

"If you didn't call about the wedding, what's up?"

Aubrey blew out a breath for courage. "I found your mother."

"No way!"

"She's here in DC."

Paul's natural cheerfulness suddenly seemed strained. "I'm happy for you, Dad. I know you've hoped for this since the last time she disappeared. How is she?"

"Not good. There's no gentle way to say this, Paul. She's dying." He'd want details. "That's all I can tell you right now." No matter how many times Aubrey repeated the news, Joanna's reappearance still seemed surreal.

"And you want me to see her? Is that why you called?"

"I can arrange it."

"I know it's the Christian thing to do. I'll be honest, Dad. I don't really care if I see her or not."

"So, you will?"

"Yeah, sure, if it makes you happy."

"What about the tour?"

"I can afford to sit a few tournaments out. I'll come home as soon as I can. The year's winding down. A break might be a good thing. Give me a chance to work on my putting. Swing's good, and I'm touted as one of the longest drivers on the European tour. If I ever hope to go stateside, I need to make more birdies."

"Four championships this year and a course record. I'd say there's probably nothing wrong with your game. You're too hard on yourself, Paul."

"Maybe."

"Let me know when you're coming home. I'm glad for your sake you'll see your mother. You won't regret that you did."

"I suppose not."

Church management often required a pastor to multi-task. As far as personal problems, Aubrey much preferred to deal with issues one at a time. Yet, during a single day, his comfortable existence had been upended.

Paul would want to know about his Uncle Gregg, as the kids used to call Fischer. "Hey, guess who's moving to Silver Spring?"

"It's too early for guessing games, Dad. Just tell me."

"Gregg Fischer."

"Neat. You two were great pals, once. Weren't you?"

Were? Perhaps Paul's question had been a prophetic one? Fischer's deception was still a mystery. Friendship required some latitude—however, Fischer had crossed the Great Meridian. "Yes, we were. Well, go back to bed. Sorry I woke you."

"Too late for apologies. Might as well face the day. Thanks for the call, Dad. I'll pray for Mother."

He hadn't asked what sickness claimed her. Paul took things in stride and played the ball wherever it landed. His faith, as pure in adulthood as a child's, helped him accept the way things were. Though wrong to envy a son, Aubrey, for whom breath itself prompted questions, wished he could accept reality as easily as his son.

One more call, the one he most dreaded. Although, perhaps a good thing in view of his recent engagement.

"Bradley? It's Dad."

"What's up? It's not Wednesday."

After this, phone calls to the children would be more sporadic. Not less frequently—rather, less predictably.

"I'm quite aware of what day it is, Bradley."

"I'm glad you called. You must have read my mind. I planned to call you tonight with my news, rather than wait until Wednesday."

"I've heard, already."

Might as well get this part over with first.

"Heard what?"

"You're getting married."

"How did you know?"

"Just got off the phone with Paul."

"Oh. Sorry. I should have let you know before this. I asked Trish only last week and she said, 'Yes.' Didn't see the need to rush with announcements. We want a very small ceremony—limited to family and a few friends. Long as I have you on the phone, would you officiate?"

Aubrey liked the brown-eyed midget Bradley had dated through his last two years of college. A good match. "Trish will make a fine addition to our family. I only hope your kids get the tall gene."

Bradley chuckled. "Come on, Dad. She seems short to you because you have to bend a little to kiss her on the cheek."

"At any rate, you have my blessing, Son. I'd be honored to officiate. Bradley—"

"Oh, yeah. You wanted to tell me something. Everybody's okay, I hope." Though generous to a fault, Bradley still held the notion the universe revolved around him.

"It's about your mother. I've found her. She's here in Silver Spring."

No response

"Bradley? Did you hear me?"

"Yeah, I heard you. I figured she'd show up sooner or later, like a bad coin."

"Don't you want to know more?"

"I suppose. Shoot."

He'd always been upfront with his children. Yet, for their sakes as well as Joanna's, caution was paramount. He shared as much as he dared and hoped Bradley's Christian sensibilities might soften his resentment. "If you want to see her, I can arrange it."

A slow, protracted sigh. "I don't think so. Thanks for telling me, though. I'll pray for her, of course. Keep me posted."

Aubrey expected resistance. He hadn't anticipated the depths of Bradley's bitterness. To push him into a different course would only make him more recalcitrant. "If you change your mind, let me know. Tell Trish I said hello and congratulations."

He'd done all he could for one night. Now, what to do about Fischer's basket of lies? Should he call Fischer tonight? No. He'd be in DC soon enough. Best to wait until then.

CHAPTER 9

Joanna squeezed "Big Blue," the five-foot stuffed bear Aubrey had brought her on his last visit, something to hold when doubts crushed her determination.

He'd said Darlene and Paul would be in to see her soon. She'd prayed for Paul's safe trip stateside. She could only imagine how they must look as adults. In her heart, she still pictured them as tiny and helpless. Aubrey tried to soften her disappointment about Bradley's resistance. "His studies keep him very busy." A mother knew when her child rejected her.

She didn't blame Bradley, nor did she deserve her children's respect. She could only hope God would soften her youngest child's heart before she passed from this world to the next.

Aubrey's attentiveness had exceeded the bounds of graciousness—his daily visits, the one happy spot in her otherwise wearisome existence. They'd read the Bible together, and he prayed for her. She had come to crave his presence more than any drug.

Sadly, she wouldn't see him again until after church services tomorrow since he had to pick up Gregg Fisher at the airport today. One more time, she had begged Aubrey to forgive Gregg for his duplicity, his actions spurred by her wishes.

"He only did what he believed friendship required," she'd told Aubrey.

In a way, she hoped he would bring Gregg by for a visit. Though Gregg would likely refuse given his deep-seated hatred toward any drug addict, let alone the one who, in his eyes, wrecked his best friend's life. Perhaps, his condemnation was well deserved. She prayed God would somehow cause her union with Aubrey to produce some fruit. At least, he'd managed to raise her children to be productive and moral adults. Was that the whole of God's plan for their marriage?

Joanna set Big Blue on the floor and reached for her mail. She'd received a few letters from Joey, with threats of bodily harm if she testified. Lucas's pressure for Joanna's testimony against Joey had intensified. He hinted he'd take away her security if she made a final refusal. Seemed she would be doomed one way or the other. How long could she put Lucas off?

What was the right thing to do? She had lived as Joey's wife, though not a legal union. She'd remained faithful, even when he slept with many other women—forced or bought or foolishly willing. Did her Christian duty require disloyalty to a murderer and criminal? The thought seemed improbable given faith's insights. She had once loved Joey, but never as she had loved Aubrey.

Until this reunion, Joey's threats failed to unnerve her. Rants meant to bring her back to him. She scanned this current letter until new words chilled her. *"Your preacher husband."* She should never have sent for Aubrey. Her selfish desire to reconcile had put him in danger. What about the children? Or her parents? So far, Joey knew nothing about her life as the daughter of a politician. What would he do if he discovered Congressman Curtis was her father? A goldmine for extortion of the worst kind, deceit that could impact more than Eastern Avenue.

The realization of her wasted life burned within. How could she have ever loved someone like Joey Juarez? Or perhaps her love for him resulted from what he gave her, a constant supply of what she'd adored the most—heroin. For as long as she lived, no one she truly loved would be safe. "Oh, God, forget my former prayer to find purpose. Keep my family safe. Take me now."

"Time for your three o'clock meds, *Señora* Beaumont."

Joanna hadn't heard the young Hispanic nurse come into her room. She must be new. Most of the attendants knocked before they entered. The girl handed her a small paper cup with three pills.

"Is Tamara off today?"

"*Sí.* I am Louisa."

The young girl avoided Joanna's inquisitive stare.

"You look familiar. Have we met before?"

"This is my first day. Perhaps you mistake me for someone else."

Louisa stood strangely still as her gaze darted about the room. Who wouldn't be nervous with armed police officers at her patient's door?

Joanna prayed daily for the hospice staff. Her peculiar circumstances must be a burden. "Well, Louisa, are you going to stand there and hold them all day, or may I have them?"

"*¿Perdón*, Señora." She handed the cup to Joanna and scooted out the door. Odd, she exited without the usual double check to make certain the patient had indeed taken all the medication.

Joanna set Big Blue on the floor. She rose with extreme effort and paced, grateful for the walker that allowed some independent mobility.

She prayed once more for eternal release. How sinful to ask God to keep her alive to perform an impossible noble task, her former prayer vain and selfish. God forgave her. As did Aubrey. These two blessings should be sufficient for an eternity of thanksgiving.

She sat on the bed as the idea brought a smile. What if God had given her a few more months of life because he wanted her to testify against Joey? Her cooperation would put an evil man behind bars where he belonged. Too many had suffered because of his maniacal ways. Tears flowed as she prayed. "If you have prolonged my life for this reason, I ask your protection for my family and to give me courage to do what is right."

She pulled back the window curtain and gazed at the circus of colors on the trees, still vibrant though most of the leaves had fallen. Not long until Thanksgiving Day. A young couple strolled along the cobbled paths, a reminder of long walks with Aubrey when they first married.

The young woman turned. Was that Louisa with the young man?

A loud rap startled her. "Come in."

"Hello, Joanna." Lucas Skylar sauntered in and helped himself to her bedside chair. Only a year her senior, his carefully groomed white hair made him appear years older.

She stared. "Well, well. If it isn't the hotshot himself."

Lucas sprawled his form with too much familiarity. He could at least pretend to be professional around her. "No need to get nasty, Joanna. I told you I wouldn't visit very often. It's too easy for me to be followed."

"What brings you here on a Saturday? Don't you have a sports game or something to attend?"

Lucas strutted around the room like a hawk circled its prey. He gave Big Blue a curiosity squeeze and sniffed her flowers, all without permission. "So where is the good Reverend Hank today?"

"You can blame the reporters for destroying his mission work. Reverend Hank has retired."

"Somehow, I would never have connected you with a minister."

"Nurse Harrington called you first, no doubt."

"Rita's a competent nurse, but she's a more valuable informant. How she loves to spill." He propped his feet on Joanna's bed, a deliberate move to annoy, no doubt.

"What do you want, Lucas? I assume this is not a social call."

"Ouch. I see your illness has not robbed you of your sauciness."

"Lucas, you're as arrogant as ever." She hoped he caught every ounce of her disdain.

He stood, then walked to the window with long, deliberate steps, pulled back the curtains, and gazed across the lawns. Though he tried to show confidence, Joanna sensed fear in his stride. His body twitched like the night she told Lucas about her pregnancy.

"Something's wrong, Lucas, terribly wrong. Tell me."

"Juarez is out on bail."

"Did you really think assault charges would hold? There's something else too."

"Another murder last night. A prostitute. Raven McNally. One of your girls, I think."

Of all her workers, Joanna had loved Raven the most. Had Joey killed her out of revenge?

"You needn't bring me more reasons why I should testify against Joey. You win, Lucas. I'll talk. Do whatever magic you must, I'm sure there's a way to preserve my testimony if I don't live long enough to appear in front of the Grand Jury. Joey's team of attorneys will postpone a trial in the hopes I don't."

Lucas's smile appeared genuine, a glimmer of sensitivity. "Good. It's the right thing to do, Joanna."

"I want protection. Not for me. For Aubrey, my children, and my parents."

"Done. We'll put a tail on them."

"I don't want them to know they're being watched."

"My agents are pros. Don't worry. By the way, we've gleaned a little information from Juarez's cellmate. Your boyfriend's not happy with you."

She smirked. "Joey has never been happy with me."

"Juarez has a contract on you. We'll do all we can to protect you."

How foolish to believe Joey might have truly loved her. He'd used her knowledge of Eastern Avenue, her girls' contacts with police and prominent politicians, to gain a stronghold. In return, he'd kept her, and her workers, supplied with drugs. "Though he's beat me more times than I can count, I never thought he'd want me dead. He is capable of tenderness, at times. I thought he loved me. Apparently, I was mistaken."

"You know too much. And love is not in Juarez's vocabulary."

"You're probably right. There was a time I craved Joey's love. Thankfully, I'm not that woman anymore."

"So you say."

"Don't you believe people can change?"

His grunt proved his true opinion of her. "I suppose some people can. You? An improbability. You ran out on Aubrey Beaumont like you ran out on me. Remember?"

"You were quite clear you wanted nothing to do with the baby."

Lucas paced. "When you dropped the load on me, I panicked. I didn't need a kid in my life. When I told you to get an abortion … I wasn't clear headed. By the time I got used to the idea, you'd disappeared. No more surprised man on earth when you turned yourself in."

She supposed love was too generic a word. With Lucas, love was a party. Aubrey loved her like a mission from God. Joey kept her for amusement. The only true human love she'd ever known came from parents she rejected. Now she belonged to Christ, a love that would never disappear. Lucas had deserved to know about Darlene. Maybe, if he knew now, he'd try harder to keep her safe—her and those Joanna loved.

"I couldn't do it, Lucas. An abortion, I mean. I wandered around Vermont for a few months. Then, I met Aubrey." She felt suddenly ashamed. "The rest you know only too well."

Lucas bolted toward her. "What are you saying? You kept the baby?"

"Congratulations, Lucas. It's a girl. I named her Darlene after your mother."

He growled like a cornered animal. Probably the first time he'd been speechless in his whole life.

"Aubrey raised her as his own, though she knows he's not her biological father."

"Does she know who I am?"

"No. Neither does Aubrey … although, I suppose he's guessed. He knows we dated right before he and I married. No one knows for sure … except you, now."

Lucas was an intelligent man, and the light bulb would shine momentarily.

"You'd be proud of our daughter. She's with the Harrowitz firm."

His eyes brightened with enlightenment. "Darlene Beaumont? My daughter? I've heard of her. Harrowitz brags on her all the time. I never made the connection to the reverend, though. Beaumont is not a common name." Lucas, never one to be floored for long, tossed Big Blue to her. "Beaumont never asked you outright if I was Darlene's father?"

She should have told Aubrey long ago. So many secrets to reveal and so little time left. "He despises you—as much as Aubrey's capable of hatred."

"Why? We've never met."

"His friend Gregg Fischer discovered you and I dated in college, and that we smoked pot together. Aubrey blames you for my drug addiction."

Lucas turned to face her, his aura somber. "We've all messed up, Joanna. The good reverend is right. I'm the one who introduced you to the stuff. We only got high a few times. I never dabbled in drugs again after college. In a way, I do feel responsible for what you became."

Lucas sorry? Something she'd thought as impossible as winter in hell. "What's done is done. Don't look to me for absolution. Only God has that power."

"God? Casey said you were religious, in constant prayer. A lot of people get chummy with the Almighty when death knocks at their door."

Whatever tenderness flickered between them burned out like a short-wicked candle. His eyes glassed over with renewed brutishness. He met her at the window. "I'll get one of the staff to help you pack."

"Now? As in this instant? At least let me call Aubrey?"

"No. Thanks to Rita, the media has had a heyday about your sentimental reunion with Beaumont. It's safer for him and you if he doesn't know where to find you."

What had she done? Did her agreement to testify mean she'd never see Aubrey again? What about the children? "Where will I go?"

Before Lucas could answer, Louisa returned. "Did you finish your medicine, Señora?"

Lucas swiveled at her voice, his countenance locked with instant recognition. "Casey. Roberts. Arrest this woman. Now."

As Joanna's guards rushed in, Louisa screamed out the window. "Run, Ramón!"

Casey and Roberts corralled Louisa just as a blizzard of shattered glass filled the room.

Lucas dropped Joanna to the floor and shielded her with his own body until the spray of bullets subsided. Roberts slipped through the window while Casey guarded the still resistive Louisa.

Lucas shook off the shards from his Lord and Taylor suit then helped Joanna to stand. "Are you alright?"

Blood oozed through her blouse at the shoulder. Strangely, she felt no pain. Shock?

The next few minutes blurred with frenzied activity, a slow-motion nightmare. Lucas played his role to perfection with all the commanding presence of his rank. Flashing lights shattered the descending darkness.

Lucas joined her in the ambulance. "How are you doing, Joanna?"

By now, the cushion of shock had worn off. "I'm sure I'll be fine once the bullet's out."

Ambulance staff started an IV and administered first aid to her wound. At the hospital, Lucas arranged for her to be put into a private room and ordered all staff to stay clear until he gave permission for her to be treated. He wrote on a notepad, *I have a plan.*

Joanna forced a smile as she wrote back. *I hope this idea works better than the last one.*

CHAPTER 10

Aubrey checked the flight arrivals. A nor'easter delayed Fischer's flight for several hours. At least his trip wasn't canceled.

Before 9/11, one could enjoy a stroll through the concourse of BWI, shop, or meander through crowds. Though limited to a sampling of stores in waiting areas, Aubrey liked to imagine people's destinations and what business took them there. An airport allowed opportunity to let fantasy take root—a microcosm of unwitting performers who scurried through life, oblivious to his interest. He'd kept his voyeuristic tendency a secret. Not everyone would understand, no matter how harmless.

His field of potential study subjects limited, the girl with the frayed cowboy hat seemed a promising diversion if his stomach would stop growling. Might as well head over to Arundel Mills, buy a book to read, and grab a cup of coffee. Maybe a donut to tide him over. He'd promised Fischer a steak dinner to celebrate his new job.

Best to muddle through a celebration, though in his heart of hearts, Aubrey was not in the mood. He still burned from his best friend's deception. What would he say when Fischer arrived? Joanna told him not to rush to judgment. For her sake, Aubrey would give Fischer a chance to explain. One didn't write off a life-long friendship any more than Aubrey could forget his marriage vows.

The mall teemed with Christmas shoppers, more opportunity to observe human nature. Though he still needed to avoid being overly friendly. Many mothers yanked their children away with petrified looks if he stopped to talk to a youngster. In Vermont, shoppers smiled at everyone, strangers as well as neighbors. In the city, few dared to make eye contact with any unknown person. To strike up a conversation with a stranger invited distrust. Although sometimes, he risked rejection if the Spirit so moved.

He missed the congeniality of small-town life. Sometimes, just for fun, he'd take a drive into the country, find a remote diner and stop. He'd listen to the friendly banter. A waitress would bring him his order and not be afraid to chat a bit.

Not so in this hodge-podge of ethnicity. He'd have to be a quiet student of this international fare of shoppers. He amused himself by observing the items people bought. The season blended so many cultural observances. Aubrey amused himself by guessing which holiday applied to the purchase.

He strolled through several neighborhoods of Arundel then drove to the nearby Book Warehouse Outlet. Other than a few Christian bookstores here and there, his favorite places to buy reading material had gone the way of the dinosaur. While here, maybe he could select a calendar as a welcome gift for Fischer. He flipped through several joke-of-the-day varieties, his snickers louder than he thought as browsers threw him disapproving stares.

"Hello, Aubrey. What's got your funny bone?" Cynthia refused to disguise her amusement. "A little far from home, aren't you?"

"I could ask you the same question." He put the calendar back on the shelf.

"Yes, you could. Deacon Yates recommended this place since it's so close to the mall. Your turn."

"My friend Fischer, the private detective who helped me locate you, arrives today. His plane was delayed, so I'm here to pass the time. I thought I'd buy a book. Can you recommend one?"

Cynthia handed him a sports almanac. "This one looks like it might appeal to your intellect. All kinds of facts in here you could quote in your sermons."

"I'm afraid you have me pegged fairly well. My children rightly criticize me for my rigidity. They want me to do at least one crazy, unpredictable thing before I die."

Aubrey thumbed through the almanac while he spoke, partly to avoid Cynthia's emerald eyes, and partly because the facts did jump out at him. "Definitely good material here."

Cynthia examined a book about famous women golfers. "And what kind of unpredictable thing would you do, if given the chance?"

"Maybe, buy that book in your hands."

She presented it to him like a gift. "Here you are. Now your children can stop nagging you."

Aubrey tucked both books under his arm. "Are you here with anyone?"

"No. I needed to get away from Dad. My father's been difficult, to say the least. I'm trying to love him—really. It's hard when he's so set in his ways."

The counselor in him could not be squelched. "Maybe we can talk over a cup of coffee."

"I believe there's a coffee shop next door, if you don't mind specialty java."

He preferred Green Mountain Roasters, perhaps more out of loyalty to his fellow Vermonters. Otherwise, he settled for simple blends. Maybe the café Cynthia suggested would have something to offer besides the exotic. He should take the opportunity to explain his sudden coolness toward her. Thanks to Rita Harrington, the rumors ran rampant. If Cynthia watched television at all, she must know Joanna had surfaced. Still, an honest explanation seemed to be the right thing.

She spotted the empty table before he did, and he followed. She ordered a latte and a blueberry turnover with a fancy name he couldn't remember. He glanced over the menu in hopes of ordering a plain cut donut. He settled for a raspberry muffin and a cup of house blend.

Cynthia gushed her frustrations with little coaxing. How she tired of Percy's unreasonable demands and how his constant care prevented her from pursuing a new circle of friends. He hadn't expected the sudden change in topic. "Aubrey, may I ask you a personal question?"

He set his cup on the table and nodded.

"Are the rumors true? Have you found your wife after all these years?"

"Most of what the media reports is based on fact. Yes. I have found Joanna. And yes, I am indeed the infamous Reverend Hank."

He'd thought the explanation might prove awkward. Instead, she accepted his unavailability with no sign of emotion. He probably overestimated her interest in him, and he in her. He enjoyed her company. Why couldn't they be friends?

Maybe she'd like to meet Fischer since his work had been instrumental in her reunion with her father. Who knows? They might prove to be good friends too. She and Fischer had a lot in common. Perhaps she wouldn't mind playing golf with two amateurs.

He pulled out his cell to check updated arrival times. "Looks like my friend's plane is due to arrive within the hour. Not many people in the church know Fischer, although he has visited a few times. I rarely speak about my personal life to congregants. He's going to bunk with me until he finds his own place."

"I'd like to meet him sometime."

"I think the two of you could be great friends."

"Aubrey, are you trying to fix me up with this man?" She picked up her purse and poised to leave.

"I'm sorry to offend you. The thought did cross my mind. Not as gallant in words as it seemed in my head."

Her face reddened. "I understand why you never asked me out. The fact you are not at liberty to pursue a relationship with me doesn't mean you are obligated to find a substitute. I can manage for myself, thank you."

He smiled. She saw right through him. "I thought, at the least, you could join Fischer and me for a round of golf on occasion."

She put her purse back on the table. "That's a possibility. I do love to golf and hate to go alone. Haven't met anyone else who enjoys the game, except for you. Is Gregg a Christian?"

"At one time, he believed as ardently as I do. In fact, I'm a Christian today because of Gregg Fischer."

"Interesting. Tell me more." She took a sip of her coffee.

"He invited me to a Campus Crusade meeting during college. Changed my life. Unfortunately, something happened that impacted Fischer's faith. Kind of like a spiritual detour."

"What was that?"

How much should a friend divulge? Since Fischer knew so much about Cynthia, only fair to even the score. "He snapped when his wife died. A crazed drug addict broke into the house. When she confronted the intruder, he sliced her open with a butcher knife."

Cynthia winced with compassion. "How terrible. Did they have any children?"

"One boy, Jason. Fischer's mother-in-law took Jason to live with her while Fischer put his life back together."

"How long ago did this happen?"

"Five years. Jason's in college now. Unfortunately, Fischer rarely sees his son except for his sporting events."

"Losing someone you love tests your faith deeply. In those hard times, it's only human to question God."

If he were to be on time for Fischer's flight, he should leave now. Funny how the minutes flew by while with Cynthia. Few activities made him forget the clock. He so enjoyed her company, and guilt riddled him. Cynthia fascinated him, an extraordinary woman who would be a haven for the right man, the kind of woman who could easily make him forget his vow to Joanna—if he were not a Christian. He could no more set aside his faith than he could his vows.

"Why not join Fischer and me for dinner? My treat."

She hesitated for only a second. "Why not? I'll follow in my car."

Gregg hoisted his carryon over his shoulders, slapped on his Orioles cap, then thanked the old geezer next to him for the pleasant conversation. The wrinkled storyteller should write a book on local folklore.

As he deplaned, he missed the days before 9/11 when family and friends waited by the gate in eager anticipation of a loved one's arrival. Even Beaumont's stiff handshake would take the sting off a bad flight.

Gregg suspected the good reverend's greeting would be colder than a North Country January. Joanna's phone call to let him know Beaumont discovered his friend's lies gave Gregg time to manufacture a plausible excuse. Joanna's explanation was truthful enough, if not the whole truth. If Beaumont thought the deception had been motivated by friendship, all the better.

Had Joanna really changed? The dying often sought God's comfort. Beaumont's New England blood, so steeped in duty and principal, required he take his wife back. Pity he gave up his pursuit of Cynthia Prescott. He deserved someone better than a floozy like Joanna.

Gregg hustled with the crowd down the long concourse to the baggage claim where Beaumont said he'd meet him. The sight of them together surprised him. So, Beaumont did start something up with Cynthia after all. Good for him.

"Fischer! Over here!" Beaumont waved his hand in the air like a hallelujah.

"Come on, you big lug, what are you afraid of?" Gregg pulled Beaumont into a resistive hug while Cynthia stifled a giggle.

"Cynthia, this is the famous, Gregg Fischer, PI."

"The one Aubrey hired to find my father. I owe you a debt of thanks. No small task, I'm certain."

The pictures didn't do her justice. Gregg tugged on his cap and tipped his head forward. "Glad to meet you, Mrs. Prescott."

"Please, call me Cynthia."

He'd never thought tall women especially attractive ... until now. She possessed an uncommon flair, athletic yet demure—an intriguing combination.

He retrieved his two large suitcases from the carousel.

"Here, let me take one." A command, not a suggestion. He liked her assertiveness, femininely shy of aggression.

"Okay, chief." As their hands touched, something more than static electricity passed between them.

"Hungry?" Beaumont always asked the obvious.

"An understatement. Don't forget you promised me a steak dinner."

"I thought we'd go to Bob's Beef Bistro. It's a sports hangout without the booze. He stopped serving alcohol because after a few drinks, people couldn't say the restaurant's name."

What'd ya know ... Beaumont told a joke. The Universe had come unglued. Gregg glanced toward the red-haired beauty. "What do you think, Cynthia?"

"Sounds good—I like steak."

Gregg stifled his surprise. With her figure, he pegged her for a rabbit-cuisine-only kind of chick.

"I'd like to get a bottle of water. They don't offer you much on the plane these days. I'm dying of thirst." As they neared the baggage area food court, an overhead television blared the local news. Beaumont and Cynthia stopped short while Gregg went on to the nearby newsstand.

"This just in—"

A broadcaster babbled about a murder at a local hospice facility. Gregg lost interest quickly. Some lowlife got axed ... big deal. In the greater Washington area, drug addicts probably got whacked all the time. Leave it to Beaumont to be drawn to a stranger's unhappy end. Sentimental to the core.

Gregg returned to find Beaumont and Cynthia in an embrace, both in tears. Gregg had left them alone for two minutes. What happened?

Beaumont faced him. "Juarez got to her, Fischer. Joanna's dead."

CHAPTER 11

No one said a word as they walked to Cynthia's car. Silence like this pained the ear worse than a jackhammer right at your feet. Cynthia and Beaumont were pretty shaken up by the news. Gregg examined his true reaction. A friend should sympathize. How awful to learn of your wife's death via a television report.

He supposed the law required next of kin be contacted before something like that gets spread all over the media. The rush to air such news came as no surprise, given the high publicity of the Juarez case. On the plus side, if there was a plus side, maybe now Beaumont could move forward. Cynthia might be the woman to restore the manhood he'd lost on Joanna.

Cynthia touched Beaumont's arm, her eyes filled with sensual compassion. Who couldn't be attracted to a woman like her? "I'm so sorry, Aubrey. We'll do dinner another time."

After she drove away, Gregg took Beaumont's keys from his hand. "I'll drive. Where are you parked?" He pointed to a black sedan parked four cars down. Of course, his car was black, as unobtrusive as the man himself.

Cynthia's goodnight was the last spoken word, and the forty-five-minute ride to the parsonage seemed anything but heavenly. Gregg worried for his friend. One thing about Beaumont, he managed sorrow head on. When his parents died, he brooded for a few days—his version of sackcloth and ashes—then came out of his funk to pay respect at their graveside as he felt duty required.

Everything related to Joanna ate at Beaumont like hydrochloric acid. No telling how he'd react now that her death was a certainty. In true Beaumont fashion, he probably convinced himself God would miraculously heal his wife. Or at the least, give him more time with her.

Gregg allowed the momentary cloud of sympathy. No time for judgments—a murdered wife, a hard memory to dispel. He fought the memories Joanna's death triggered. Frozen snapshots he'd buried for so long. Blood everywhere. Marla's eyes fixed as if to ask, "Why weren't you here to save me?"

They'd argued at breakfast over Marla's extravagant purchase of a top-of-the-line handbag. She'd cajoled him. "Terrific sale," she'd said. He'd argued the bag would've been cheaper if she'd never bought the ugly thing.

He'd stormed out of the house when she started to cry. If it would bring her back, he'd buy every handbag in Brattleboro.

He'd stopped going to church. Not because he lost his belief in God. Marla's death left him to drift on a sea of doubt without his spiritual anchor. He supposed while at Beaumont's, church would naturally be on the agenda.

Beaumont seemed to come out of his self-imposed silence as Gregg pulled into the driveway. "We're here." Gallant Beaumont exited the car first then took one of Gregg's duffle bags. "I've made up a bed for you in the downstairs guest room at the back of the house. Should be quiet. I thought you'd like the room with the television."

Gregg followed Beaumont through the garage entryway and then through the main living room. Every chair and fixture seemed the same. Beaumont didn't like to rearrange anything. "Make yourself at home. Oh, are you hungry? I'll make us a couple of sandwiches while you get settled in."

Gregg threw the car keys on the nightstand. "Don't worry about me, buddy. I know where everything is."

Beaumont nodded and shuffled off toward his study while Gregg unpacked … in under fifteen minutes. Might as well give his host a little more time to brood before joining him in the kitchen.

Or maybe he needed time to brood as well. Joanna's death brought too many memories, Marla's murder—a grief too long repressed. He put his Glock and revolver in the nightstand and found the Bible Beaumont kept in the drawer—the one he'd given Beaumont when they were in college. He picked it up and read the inscription:

To: Aubrey
From: Gregg
May you find the Source of Life in these pages

Gregg leaned back on the bed and flipped to Romans, the book he'd used to lead Beaumont to Christ, searching those same Scriptures now for words of comfort, what a good friend should do. Funny that he would pray for Beaumont's peace when Gregg himself still ranted against Marla's death. Maybe the time had come for him to seek his own healing before he prayed for someone else. He slipped to his knees like the prodigal he was. Ironic that the woman he most despised, in death was the catalyst to bring him back to the God he loved.

Cynthia flipped on the entryway light. "Dad, I'm home!"

No response. She gazed into the living room. No surprise here. Dad sat in the dark, his eyes glued to the television, and the volume cranked to full.

She placed her purchases on the counter and hung her coat in the closet then sorted through the unopened mail Dad left on the table. She fumed at the final notice from the power company. Dad's finances were a mess. He refused her help. "I can manage my own affairs, little girl."

Pity was, he couldn't.

If nothing changed, she'd have to file for guardianship, an infringement against his independence, the least preferred option. What else could she do? He refused to give her power of attorney, and she'd go broke if she continued to pay his bills behind his back.

Apparently, he hadn't heard her come in.

She flung the newest batch of past due notices on the tray table in front of him.

"Dad, I said I'm home. Did you eat, yet? Probably not. No dishes in the sink or on the tray table next to his recliner. He looked like he hadn't moved since she'd left. Given the faint urine smell, he probably didn't get up to go to the bathroom either.

The social worker had warned the dementia would worsen, that his home care needs would present challenges beyond her means and patience to endure. The social worker had also recommended that Dad stay in the hospital while he waited for a vacancy in a residential care facility. Cynthia hoped the time spent caring for him at his home might help bridge the years apart. What possessed her to try? "Do you want ham or turkey for your sandwich?"

He turned to face her. "Hello, Cynthia. I never heard you come in. How was your day?"

Terrible, Dad.

"I bought you a couple of books to read. I know you like Westerns. And I picked up a sixteen-month calendar too. One you can start using now instead of waiting until January. Where would you like me to hang it?"

"Any place is fine."

Would he bother to look at it?

"Could you make me a bologna sandwich?"

Bologna. Always Bologna. "A steady diet of bologna can't be healthy for anyone. You are supposed to watch your salt. Why don't I heat up the chicken soup the church ladies sent over?"

Dad waggled his finger at her. "I'm pleased as pie you're here with me, but I don't want ya changin' everythin'. Just get me a bologna sandwich like I asked. That's a good girl."

She put two pieces of bologna between two slices of bread. Nothing else—the way her father liked it—dry and undressed. Yuck. She set the sandwich on the tray in front of him. Sometimes she wished Aubrey Beaumont hadn't been so persuasive. His sentimental arguments had resonated—she should try to restore a relationship with her father while he still remembered who she was. What relationship? How does somebody repair a relationship where one never existed? She'd lived most of her life in ignorance of the man who'd sired her. Her mother thought he probably died. Or maybe she only wished he had, although she never remarried. Cynthia had prayed that one day she'd find her father. Instead, she'd discovered a cantankerous old man.

"Hold on to your senses, Cynthia," she muttered under her breath. The adjustment couldn't have been easy for Dad, either. He was still a babe in Christ. Dementia didn't help. According to the counselor, irritability was a normal part of the progression—symptoms of illness, not of a soul far from God. A shame they found one another when dementia had robbed him of what little the liquor left.

She strained to remember the man she used to call Daddy, that part of him perhaps gone forever. Gratefully so. A drunken man who abused his wife. Did a real father now exist somewhere within his damaged brain?

She muted the television. "Dad, can we talk? I need to tell you something about Pastor Aubrey."

He patted the couch, his tone gentler. "Come sit here. The football game can wait." Hope rebirthed as he consciously turned off the television.

She relayed how she'd run into Aubrey earlier, and her father listened, as much as a demented ninety-year-old could. She told him of her initial attraction. "It's no use. Aubrey is emotionally incapable of a romantic relationship, especially now."

"Why not?"

"His estranged wife was brutally murdered today. I'm surprised you didn't know. It's been all over the news. Of course, you only watch the sports channel."

Dad moved his jaw back and forth as if he chewed on her report. He took her hand in his, a precious moment of true affection. He stroked her hair with shrunken, gnarled hands once strong and huge. She recalled how her daddy of long ago could be tender and kind when sober. "Sometimes life comes at us hard, little girl. And we think God ain't fair. I'm only beginnin' to see God's ways are not ours."

Out of the mouth of babes ...

Compassion for his pastor mirrored in Dad's eyes. "Is he all alone now? Seems like somebody ought to be with him."

"His friend is there, the investigator—the one who found me. He's moved to DC to start a new job and will stay with Pastor Aubrey until he gets his own place. I had invited them both for dinner tomorrow before we heard about Pastor Aubrey's wife."

She hesitated to say more. Could she trust this near stranger with her deepest unholy feelings? "Dad, I don't know how to pray. I should feel sorry for his pain. In some ways, I do. Selfishly, I'm almost glad she's gone. She was his albatross."

"I see," his quizzical grin an enigma.

"Not because I want him for myself."

"Reverend Beaumont's not the man for you, Cindy."

How could he know what kind of man his daughter needed? "You're right, of course."

"God has someone in mind. Ya gotta be patient." He squeezed her hand in his weakness, yet with the strength of love.

"I'm so tired of being alone."

"When you got Jesus, you ain't never alone."

As if his mind flicked a switch, he turned the television back on.

Thanks, Dad. For a cantankerous old coot, you're not so dumb.

CHAPTER 12

Gregg tiptoed into the kitchen. Beaumont had set the table with two ham and cheese sandwiches, fruit cocktail, and a carafe of coffee. "I'm glad to see you set a place for yourself."

"I don't really want to eat, but I'll try to get down a few bites. You'll pester me until I do." He took a sip of coffee. "I planned on grocery shopping tomorrow." He went to the cupboard and brought out a boxed chocolate cake. "All I have to offer for dessert."

Gregg twirled the cake around. "Don't see any mold on it. Guess it's safe." He sat and gulped his coffee. "At least you still make a great cup of coffee."

Beaumont offered a small smile and took a bite of his sandwich. He set it down as he oozed a heavy sigh. "What do I do now, Fischer?"

"You're still in shock. You should rest."

"I should call the children, I suppose. Paul's expected to be here late tomorrow night. I'll try his cell. He'll crash with Bradley. The boys and I hoped to meet Darlene for dinner Wednesday night to celebrate Bradley's engagement. Shame they didn't get here before …"

He balled his fists and pounded the table. "I should have been there to protect her. I failed her again."

The one thing Gregg could do was sway Beaumont away from undeserved and purposeless guilt. "Don't go there, Beaumont. I've pinged myself upside the head at least a hundred times tonight as I asked myself, the question—what if I'd told you the truth when I first saw Joanna— would that have changed anything? So maybe, in a way, I'm responsible."

Beaumont laid his palms on the table. "No, Fischer, you're not. I forgive you for your secretiveness. Joanna explained how she made you promise not to tell me. A promise is a promise. Later, she became a Christian. Who knows? If I'd barged in like Sir Galahad, would she have come to the Lord?"

Hard to believe someone like her would find her way to Christ. "True, I never liked her. I'm still sorry. She didn't deserve to be murdered."

"Does anyone?" Beaumont brought over his wedding picture from the fireplace mantel. "I hate this helpless feeling. How did you get over the pain after Marla died?"

Gregg leaned back in his chair. What small iota of encouragement could he give Beaumont on that score? "You never truly get over the hollowness. You go on. You have your faith. As for me, I refused God's help when I needed him the most. Don't make the same mistake I did."

"Thanks. That means a lot coming from you."

"Well, maybe this time, I'll pray for you."

Beaumont raised an inquisitive eyebrow.

"Yeah. I think the Big Guy and me are getting back on track."

"About time." Beaumont chowed down his supper and gulped down the rest of his coffee. He cut the cake and served Gregg first. "Surprised I was able to eat."

"I'm sure food's what the doctor ordered. Nothing like a piece of pie or cake to clear your head. You've got a lot of decisions to make."

"What are my rights, Fischer? Technically, I'm still Joanna's husband. Can I claim her body and give her a decent funeral? I'll give Lucas Skylar a call."

Good. A mission. Exactly what the man needed. When the pain ebbed, perhaps he'd remember Cynthia and move on.

CHAPTER 13

Lucas chewed his lower lip. What could he tell a man of the cloth? Deceit came easily to him; however, he disliked the feast of lies he had thrown to Beaumont. "Sorry, Reverend Beaumont. You can't claim Joanna's body."

"I'm her husband."

"She had no next of kin listed, and technically she was in our custody. Her body was released to Rolling Greens Funeral Home for cremation not more than two hours ago. Perhaps if you contact them—"

"I will."

Good, he bought the story. Lucas had known only a handful of clergy and had lumped them into two categories—piously phony or fools. Beaumont fit neither. His anger touched a nerve. Was he still in love with her after everything Joanna had put him through? She wouldn't live more than a few weeks, two months at the most. At least if Juarez thought the hit successful, he'd leave Beaumont and Joanna's children alone. Best plan for all concerned.

Best to be certain Beaumont didn't accidentally discover the truth. Lucas punched the number for Rolling Greens. He'd paid Burt Cummings enough for the cover up. He'd better come through convincingly.

Joanna threw the paper across the room. Casey had stepped outside to give her a much-needed private moment to digest the falsified news report of her untimely demise. Except the brief mention of her marriage to Reverend Aubrey Beaumont, the recount read like a rap sheet. Thankfully, Lucas kept her connection to Congress out of the papers.

Lucas demanded too much of her. There must be another way. She never trusted him when they dated. Why should she put her life in his hands now? He had his sights on the Maryland State Legislature. A win on this case would cement his election next year. He'd help her stay alive as long as necessary to achieve his goal. Then he'd abandon her, as he did the day she told him about her pregnancy. He must believe this plan would work. Lucas took few risks. Rattlesnakes strike for protection, not malice.

Condemnation proved pointless. How could she seek forgiveness from others when she herself had yet to forgive Lucas?

All these years she'd let him believe she'd agreed to the abortion.

What would he do now? Would he own up to an illegitimate child? Maybe the scandal wouldn't kill his political aspirations as such disgrace might have in the past. It was a different world these days, where deeds of unrighteousness were heralded as courageous. Might even raise his approval rating.

At the least, he should be pleased he'd sired another legal eagle and take pride in Darlene's accomplishments. For her sake, he should not disrupt her life any further.

Lucas was right about one thing. Joey would lose interest in Aubrey if he thought his mistress was dead and could no longer rat on him. What harm could a Silver Spring preacher do to Joey's Eastern Avenue kingdom? Aubrey's career as Reverend Hank had ended, and the hapless do-gooder was nothing but a dissipated cloud on Joey's parade.

As well as a chance to protect her family, perhaps this ridiculous scheme was God's answer to her prayer. If so, the seclusion was almost bearable. Lucas's precautions were carried out to the extreme. Her nurse insisted she be in bed by ten as if she were a child. She took advantage of these few moments of privacy while she changed into her nightclothes and used the time to reorder her frustrations into purpose. She fastened her robe and knelt by her bed. Prayer still seemed awkward to her, yet her paltry efforts never failed to bring peace. Maybe God didn't care as much about the how. Rather, he responded most to a sincere heart.

Aubrey had always ended his prayers with an Amen. He said the word meant, "So be it," a kind of reaffirmation, a belief God had heard the petition, a mental over and out as well as God's roger that and stand by.

She pulled herself up from the floor and stretched on her bed, exhausted from the simple act of humility before God. How soon before she could no longer pray on her knees?

The door opened, and Lucas barged in. "Tomorrow, you'll be moved north. Remember. No phone calls. The world thinks Joanna Beaumont is dead. Best to keep the ruse going. You need anything more tonight?"

"I'm fine. Frick and Frack can come in now. And, don't worry, I'll be a perfect little stool pigeon for you. By the way, thanks for keeping Casey and Roberts assigned to me. I know you called in a few favors to keep them on."

"Roberts wasn't too thrilled. Casey likes you. For local cops, they're as good as any FBI agents." Lucas shouted by the door. "Come on in, fellows. Bluebird awaits."

"Hardly an ingenious code name, Lucas. Bluebirds are overrated symbols. They crap on clothes like any other bird."

Lucas sneered. "And what fowl friend would you like to be called?"

"I like falcons. They give chase to their prey."

Like a revolving door, Lucas left, then Casey and Roberts entered.

"Good evening, Miss Joanna." Casey picked the paper off the floor, folding and placing it on her bedside table. "Somethin' in the news upset you?"

Her guard seemed always ready with a smile regardless of his charge's tempers. "You have the gift of understatement, Casey. The room is so small I'm apt to die of suffocation before the cancer does me in."

"Try to get some rest. Roberts and I will be as quiet as church mice."

She wanted to talk, not sleep. Roberts rarely spoke; Casey talked enough for the two of them and blamed his verbiage on his Irish heritage.

"Casey, are you married?"

"I am, Miss Joanna."

"For how long?"

"Going on thirty-five years, now."

"Happy years?"

His paunchy stomach rolled with his laugh. "Mostly."

"Kids?"

"Six—and fourteen grandchildren."

"Whew."

"Yeah. Christmas is a zoo at our house."

Thanksgiving and Christmas fast approached. After she left Aubrey, holidays were simply another day to get high. Would she live long enough to see them through Christian eyes? Would it be selfish to ask for one more Christmas with family before she left this earth? Or to see her son married? She sighed at the losses—never to hold a grandchild on her lap.

Casey sat in the chair next to the motel dresser. "I know we're not supposed to ask personal questions."

"You can ask me anything, Casey. I trust you." He seemed more like a jolly older brother than a guard.

"Do you know Jesus, Miss Joanna?"

"Absolutely, though only recently."

No surprise Casey would witness to his charge. A blessing to have someone near who shared her faith. Like a human guardian angel. "Would you like me to pray with you?"

More than she deserved. "Thank you."

Roberts groaned. "Sappy."

Casey ignored his partner's displeasure. "You don't have to listen."

"Fine. While you two dial-up heaven, I'll go out for a smoke."

Casey shrugged his shoulders, then knelt by his chair. He prayed for everyone's safety.

Joanna inhaled the gift of peace that filled the room. Though the rest of her days depended upon the wisdom of ungodly men, God still cared for her soul.

When back in his room, Gregg punched in his direct number to Congressman Curtis.

The congressman sighed like a broken man. "I'd hoped the news had been wrong. I'd hoped she'd turn around, find us, let us enjoy our grandchildren."

"I'm sorry for your loss."

"I appreciate your efforts, Mr. Fischer. You will continue to keep me informed about my grandchildren?"

"Of course."

"There'll be a check in the mail tomorrow. What address will you use now?"

Perhaps he should set up an online account or post office box in DC. Might take a while before he found an apartment and best not to receive the congressman's payment at Beaumont's. "Send a cashier's check to my new office for now."

CHAPTER 14

Cynthia pulled out the inexpensive dinnerware she'd bought at the mall a few days before. She wearied of using her father's glued plates. At least she'd have decent dinnerware to set on the table this afternoon.

She checked the pot roast. Done. Now to keep things warm until Gregg arrived. Apparently, punctuality didn't hold the same importance for him as for Aubrey.

The cell jarred her from her thoughts as she read the text from Gregg: *On my way. Be there ASAP. Have stop to make.*

Too bad Aubrey was unable to come. Odd about the emergency board meeting the elders called for this evening. With the lukewarm handshakes he received after church, he might appreciate a break in the madness. His passionate sermon this morning, although a nice detour from his usual dry lecture, alarmed her. As if he sensed something in the wind.

She replied to Gregg's text then set the cell back on the table. As if in a daze, she took the salad ingredients out of the refrigerator and chopped while her mind wandered, amazed at God's meticulous timing—how he'd brought Gregg to Silver Spring when Aubrey most needed a friend.

Would dinner with Gregg seem awkward without Aubrey? She welcomed any company these days, and Dad behaved better around other men. She followed sports and tried to engage Dad in whatever he was watching on ESPN. He tuned her out. The social worker thought company would be good stimulation for Dad. *Good therapy for me too.*

With the doorbell's chime, Cynthia's face heated like a schoolgirl's first date. Odd sensation. Attraction? So soon after her disappointment over Aubrey? Could be what she thought was attraction had merely been admiration.

Gregg held out a bouquet of red roses like a toddler offers his mother a handful of dandelions. "These are for you."

"Thank you." She inhaled their fragrance. "They're beautiful. Come in, dinner's almost ready."

"Need help? I'm not very handy in the kitchen, but I can shuffle plates around." He glanced at the preset table. "Looks like you already have everything under control." His boyish smile matched his mischievous wink. "Maybe I'll join Percy in the living room."

"I'll introduce you. Don't be upset if he's forgotten you met him at church today. He has Alzheimer's."

"Beaumont told me."

She tapped her father on his shoulder. "Dad, Gregg Fischer is here."

"Nice to meet you, Gregg. Name is Percy Logan."

"Gregg is the private investigator Pastor Aubrey hired to find me."

Dad offered Gregg a handshake. She remembered how a neighbor once described her father as a pleasant drunk. Was there such a thing?

Dad returned his attention to the television. "Do you like hockey?"

"Sure do. My son plays."

"You're welcome to watch the game with me."

"Don't mind if I do."

Cynthia smiled as Gregg relaxed on the sofa, drawn to the television like her third graders to a Disney flick. "I'll call when dinner's ready."

Gregg and Dad raised their hands and cheered in unison. "He scores."

As Gregg watched the game with Percy, he wondered if Jason might be playing a game today. "So, who's your favorite team, Percy?"

He laughed. "Montreal. Don't tell my daughter. She favors the Blackhawks."

"Not surprised, since she's from Chicago. So, you're quite the hockey fan, hey?"

Percy snickered. "Like golf more. What about you, Gregg?"

"I like hockey. My son plays for his college team. I hit the greens on occasion. My favorite sport, though, is baseball."

"Seen my share of interesting baseball games. The Cubs. When I lived in Chicago."

Cynthia's two-minute warning came from the kitchen as loud as a foghorn. "Everything's ready. Come and eat before the salad gets warm and the potatoes get cold."

"Let's eat, boy." Percy said as he led the way into the dining room. Without missing a beat, he carried on the conversation as he sat down. "I was born in the Washington area. My father took me to all the games. My father used to talk about the seventh game in the 1924 World Series. Why, you could hear 'em shoutin' all the way to Baltimore when Washington won in the twelfth. My father took off when I was eight. Guess that memory of his stuck with me."

Cynthia motioned for Gregg to take a chair opposite Percy. Gregg added his bit of knowledge. "They blew the series the next year. Lost to the Pirates."

"That a fact. What are you, a sports encyclopedia?"

The old salt might not have much recent memory. At least, he maintained a briny wit.

Cynthia seemed to be in tune with their conversation. Rare to find a gal so up on sports history. "Good dinner, Cynthia. Home-cooked meals are a treat. Beaumont's a fair cook when he has time. Most often, we order in or eat out."

"Say, I'd like seconds on those potatoes, Cindy girl." Percy winked. "Ya know, for a college kid, my little girl sure can cook."

Cynthia passed the potatoes and met Gregg's stare. "I like baseball too. I think the most memorable game I ever saw was with my late husband. We had tickets to the sixth World Series game between the Mets and the Red Sox. The Mets fought hard all year. It didn't look promising when the Sox led 5-3 in the bottom of the tenth. The Mets would have lost if the Sox hadn't gotten cocky. Buckner let a ball roll between his legs, and the Sox lost. Funny how one small mistake can change history."

While attempting to find her, Gregg had collected a huge dossier on Cynthia Prescott, and he probably knew more about her than he'd known about his wife. He knew Cynthia's favorite color was blue and that she drove around the block as many times as needed to find a parking spot where she didn't have to parallel park. Yet, he hadn't appreciated her intellect until this moment.

Beaumont would be one lucky man if he landed Cynthia. Oh, he'd be torn up about Joanna for a while. Gregg looked at Cynthia in a way a man should not gaze at a best friend's girl. He loved the very thought of her, how she took a little hiccup with each breath, and the way she chewed her nails when Percy said something to upset her, which he seemed to do about every other sentence.

Gregg sighed. This attraction niggled at his conscience. Wrong on so many levels. He should beg his leave and keep his distance. "Thanks again for dinner, Cynthia. I really should be going."

"Won't you stay for dessert?"

He wished he could stay for the rest of his life.

"I should see how Beaumont's doing."

"He loved Joanna a great deal. He told me so."

"And you understand?" More than remarkable, to put her own attraction aside to let Beaumont grieve.

"I consider Aubrey a friend too, you know."

"Friend? I thought—"

"Thought what?"

He hesitated, not sure of how to answer. The moment grew increasingly awkward.

"Don't tell me you thought Aubrey and I were—involved?"

Gregg coughed to disguise his embarrassment. "The thought crossed my mind."

"I admire Aubrey very much, but I don't think either of us are interested in anything more. Even if there were love between us, Joanna's death won't free him from her hold on him."

For once in his life, Gregg was glad to be dead wrong. "I suppose I could stay a little longer. Apple pie's my favorite."

CHAPTER 15

Aubrey unlocked the church office, another layer of security he despised. His heart pounded with prophetic anxiety. He needed the extra half hour to pray and think, the church usually his refuge in times of worry. Why did he feel like a tree about to be felled?

Had the elders gathered to simply reprimand him again or would they finally ask for his resignation? He'd tired from the probes, the nonsensical questions of the curious. From the moment Rita Harrington made her first phone call, paparazzi camped at the parsonage doorstep and now, the hallowed grounds of the church. At first, reporters pried into every intimate detail of his life. They asked how Joanna's death affected his work and what plans had he made for her final arrangements. Why must media crawl inside his grief, expose his sorrows for profit? Weren't there fires and tornados to report?

Joanna's lover murdered her to forever silence her. Any information he might have about Joey Juarez had been hearsay. Why this continued fascination? Drug addicts died every day, and few cared about Joanna as the wife Aubrey loved.

His solitude ended as Deacon Yates entered. "Hello, Pastor Aubrey. Sorry we called this meeting on short notice. I know you've got a lot on your mind right now. We're sorry for your loss."

Aubrey accepted the deacon's handshake, though his words fell flat with insincere undercurrents, lacking even a pretense of warmth. His text before Sunday service came as no surprise—the publicity probably as upsetting to the congregation as to their pastor. Aubrey sensed the elders' disapproval in their rigid, plastic faces while he preached.

Only a few offered sincere well wishes—Cynthia, Percy, and Fischer among them. Most passed by in timid recognition and granted a polite nod before they stepped clear of the reporters perched at the doors. Some welcomed the opportunity for national attention and smiled broadly as the cameras rolled. Aubrey had noticed Deacon Yates's scowl and overheard his remark to his wife. "This can't be tolerated any longer."

The quiet at the conference table fouled the air as board members filed in, sans the usual gossip before the call to order. Major Hale Barnett sat across from Sergeant Jim Lacy, mirror images of military decorum. Jeanette

Peters, who missed six out of the last seven meetings, must have felt the firing of a pastor something of importance. Jonas Jackson, the sole African American member of the board, scoured the room with disdain. Aubrey counted. Every elder was present, an attendance record.

Deacon Yates called the meeting to order. "Pastor Aubrey, there's no easy way for us to approach this delicate matter. So, I'll out with our thoughts the best I can."

Jonas Jackson stood. "I want you to know, pastor, I voted against this decision." He glared at Deacon Yates and sank back into the chair.

Deacon Yates continued. "Thank you for your thoughts, Brother Jonas. We appreciate your insights. The rest of us, Pastor Aubrey, are very concerned about these recent matters regarding your ex-wife."

Aubrey suppressed a grin. "I'm sorry for any distress my personal life may have caused the members. For the record, Joanna and I are … were … technically married. You knew my marital status when you hired me."

Deacon Yates cleared his throat. "We knew you were separated from your wife. We didn't know about her … um … connections. This reflects badly on our church. You do understand, don't you?"

"I understand you are afraid that my wife's past drug addiction soils the church's reputation."

"There's more."

"I suspected as much." His smirk probably did little to help his cause.

"While your wife's association with a known drug lord alarms us, we are more taken aback over this street ministry you organized without church approval. We should have at least been informed."

Deacon Yates placed a copy of Aubrey's hiring contract on the table. "According to this, we have the right to call a vote of confidence by the congregation whenever a pastor's integrity or moral conduct is called into question. A favorable vote would override this body's recommendation of termination."

They caught him in a vice. If he requested the vote of confidence, the church would split regardless of the outcome. Such an action would hurt his flock far more than if he resigned. Deacon Yates probably counted on their pastor's unwillingness to be the source of dissension. Aubrey stiffened. "I assume there is a letter."

Deacon Yates sifted through the contents of a manila folder and produced a sealed envelope addressed to *The Reverend Aubrey Beaumont.*

"It's with sincere regret I give this to you. You'll notice the letter is personally signed by all the elders except for Jonas, of course."

Aubrey tore open the envelope and read the sugar-coated request for his immediate resignation. He loved these people, the elders included, albeit was impatient with their narrow mindedness. He stoically returned the official record to the envelope. This dismissal, though not technically defined as termination, was simply another failure in his long list of demolished dreams. "You needn't worry, Deacon Yates. You'll have my resignation by tonight. I'll vacate the parsonage as soon as possible. Is that satisfactory?"

All nodded except for Jonas Jackson, whose eyes filled with tears.

"Is there any other business, Deacon Yates?"

"No, Reverend Beaumont. We do want to say how deeply we regret this development. You are still well thought of. The board has agreed to provide you with a letter of reference."

Aubrey put both hands on the table. "You can be assured there are no hard feelings on my part, Deacon Yates. Good night."

They exited faster than Monday night at the Bingo hall. Only Jonas lingered, unashamed of his moistened cheeks. When everyone else left, Aubrey approached his solitary advocate.

"Anything you need, Pastor Aubrey, you call me. Okay?" When Jonas left, Aubrey faced the night alone.

Though he had sensed the nature of this summons, foreknowledge did little to soften the blow against his ego. He needed to think before he went home … no, no longer his home … merely a place to crash for a few more days. Where could he walk without the constant bombardment of the news zoos?

He strolled through the courtyard prayer garden, the pride of the Martha Ministries and the Men's Fellowship. Shrubs, trees, and plants, each labeled with its biblical importance and Scripture references, arrayed the cobbled path, a place where a confused soul could ponder what to do next. In the middle of the garden stood a small covered chapel furnished with a padded bench, altar rail, and candles. Near the bench, a stack of bibles was replenished daily.

Aubrey found the beauty of the Prayer Garden ironically a source of comfort. While he had supported the project, he suggested they build a similar spot on Eastern Avenue. The motion was quickly defeated.

Tonight, however, the serenity of this place soothed his riled spirits. He mourned Joanna's death more than he mourned her abandonment. He'd spent the early part of the afternoon in contemplation of a memorial on her behalf. Some sort of goodbye. Skylar's hurried cremation came as no surprise. At least he allowed Aubrey to collect Joanna's ashes. Where would she want them scattered? Stowe?

Perhaps he should visit her parents. They might want to have a say in the matter.

He'd hoped the walk would bring peace. Instead he'd wandered through the senselessness of the last week. Was his ministry over? Or did the Lord have another plan? Why did God bring Joanna back to him only to allow this violent end? She'd prayed her witness against her former lover might bring a purpose for her suffering. How could a loving heavenly Father ignore her last request and let Juarez walk free?

Aubrey brushed off the ice crystals from his coat. Might as well continue his prayers in the warm parsonage before he called Joanna's estranged parents. To Aubrey's knowledge, they'd lost all contact with her. If he called, they might refuse to speak with him. Even so, contacting Congressman Curtis and his wife was the right thing to do.

Aubrey shivered. He should have turned on the furnace before he went to the board meeting. At least, he was sheltered from the rain. A slight cough annoyed him. Water might help. He ambled into the kitchen. He grabbed a clear crystal glass and stared in unusual fascination as it filled to overflowing. Simple physics—the theory of displacement. The old made room for the new. He turned off the faucet, then raised the glass, mesmerized by the play of light on the water's surface. He smiled, not at anything pleasurable, for his spirit still ached. As he studied the miracle, he sensed himself on the water traveling from one side of his pain to the other, from confusion to clarity. Assurance filled him. Joanna's death would not be in vain.

CHAPTER 16

Aubrey followed the aged butler as he led the way into the inner sanctum of Washington royalty. Careful of his steps, Aubrey dared to glance at the crystal and jade ornaments displayed on mahogany shelves, a prelude to the opulence that graced the centuries-old mansion.

"Reverend Beaumont, Madam," the butler announced. He offered a courteous nod, then left as Mrs. Curtis gestured toward a leather side chair. Aubrey fidgeted as he sat, unable to find a comfortable position. He surrendered to the unforgiving cushions and leaned back. He smiled inwardly at the propensity of the rich to prefer style over ease.

"Thank you for coming, Aubrey."

"I felt the time had come for us to meet in person."

He had grown up with financial security, his mother a successful commercial artist and his father a dentist. He had never known want. As an adult, God more than met his temporal needs. Now, gazing upon splendor he could never imagine, he felt impoverished.

Aubrey chewed his lower lip with sudden anxiety. Were his motives for this visit as noble as he thought? Or had he selfishly believed he could build a bridge to Joanna through her parents?

Harold "Butch" Curtis, fourth generation to serve in the United States Congress, possessed a long and powerful run in politics. Joanna had been his only child, and none of the grandchildren held political ambitions. Was he the last in line of a great family?

Congressman Curtis sat on the davenport, a lump of silence compared to his wife, the real force behind his long career. Although he stood more than a foot taller than Mrs. Curtis, Aubrey felt dwarfed in the presence of the "Queen of the Beltway."

How much would Joanna have resembled her mother if she had lived to age gracefully like Mrs. Curtis, a woman with an enviable figure and a youngish face who defied her ninety-three years?

"Sugar?"

She never asked if he wanted tea. She assumed he'd accept, and one did not argue an assumption made by Madeline Curtis.

"Two lumps. No cream."

Aubrey fought the sudden queasiness. Like the brooms in Fantasia, the little cinnamon sticks tucked uniformly in the chalice of the Wallace tea set leapt to life. They danced in choreographed mockery.

Mrs. Curtis must have sensed his uneasiness. "Are you all right, Aubrey?"

"Yes. I'm embarrassed. I have an aversion to cinnamon." There. He confessed his quirk, and the first to hear of his weakness, the mother of its source.

"We'll dispense with these immediately. Rosa!"

She appeared like one beamed from a starship, an immediate response to the buzzer on the side of Madeline Curtis's chair. She handed Rosa the offensive cinnamon sticks. "Take these away." No explanation. She simply gave an order with unmitigated expectation she would be unquestioningly obeyed.

"There," she said as Rosa left. "I appreciate your honesty, Aubrey." She scowled at her husband. "Most men are too timid to admit frailty of any kind." She passed Aubrey his tea as she gazed at him. Was this his cue to speak?

What could he say?

With practiced congeniality, she prodded Aubrey into conversation. "I must tell you, Aubrey, we were a bit surprised you wanted to see us. We hadn't heard from Joanna since she left college; she was always a rebellious child. At the time, she was dating Lucas Skylar, then she fell off the radar. Except for the birth announcements you sent us, we would not have known we had grandchildren. Thank you, by the way, for the lovely letter of invitation to Bradley's wedding."

Aubrey shifted his weight from one hip to another as he precariously balanced his tea cup. "I wanted to extend sympathy. I donated a sum of money to the nursing home where she stayed. Though she wasn't there long, the staff was very good to her. They have set up a plaque in her honor. I thought you should know."

Mrs. Curtis softened. "A wonderful idea. We'll be sure to send a donation as well. We plan to erect a memorial stone in our family burial plot. What are your plans for her ashes?"

"I hope to disperse them over Stowe Mountain. I don't know when yet. Probably not until after Bradley's wedding."

"Why Stowe? That's your right, of course. And the area is beautiful. We have been there in the past."

"Joanna and I were married at Stowe and had a short honeymoon there."

Mrs. Curtis's eyes filled with tears, perhaps a mother's pain for not being able to attend her only child's wedding.

Aubrey set his tea on the marbled-top end table. "I'm sure my visit is awkward for all of us."

Congressman Curtis met Aubrey's gaze. "Please, believe us when we say we loved Joanna as much as any parent loves their child. Though we weren't as old as Abraham and Sarah, she was born to us in later years, and I fear we spoiled her."

Aubrey pushed judgment aside. They'd lost an estranged daughter with no hope of reconciliation. Their grief must at least match his.

Congressman Curtis cleared his throat. "You might say Joanna was a casualty of war … a war of political collusion. Washington is a cruel place for children of powerful parents. Several of our colleagues have lost a child to addiction."

Mrs. Curtis joined in her husband's defense. "Joanna's problems did not surface until after she left for college. As a child, though rebellious and spirited, she never gave us significant cause to worry. How does a parent predict what course a child's life will lead? We tried to contact her after you sent us Darlene's birth announcement. She refused to take our call. We wrote, and she returned the letters unopened."

"I didn't know you had a desire to see the children, Mrs. Curtis. I'm so sorry. Joanna led me to believe you and the congressman wanted nothing to do with her or us."

"We never understood her rejection, although she may have had misguided reasons. Joanna expressed her love in odd ways."

The congressman nodded. "Joanna inherited her mother's indomitable will. I'm certain you have tasted Joanna's stubbornness. Right or wrong, we ultimately decided to respect her wishes."

At first glance, one might label Madeline Curtis an enigma, at ease in her environment as if born to serve tea and converse with strangers. Yet, her willingness to write Joanna off seemed an affectation. Mrs. Curtis's taut presence defied sensibility. What were they not telling him?

Congressman Curtis leaned forward, perhaps about to reveal a painful truth. "We are not monsters, Aubrey. Joanna's death has affected us deeply.

Through the years, we uttered many prayers to be reconciled with our daughter."

Aubrey paled in unchecked resentment. Why hadn't the Lord answered this unselfish prayer?

Congressman Curtis clasped his hands together. "That we are people with enormous influence is no secret. Since Joanna refused to have anything to do with us, we found a trustworthy person who has kept us informed about you and the children."

Aubrey stiffened as he handed Mrs. Curtis his teacup. "If I may, I think I will have another cup."

She poured a fresh supply into a clean cup, then passed it to him. "After Joanna left you the last time, our source advised us she'd gone underground and became involved in a prostitution ring. Nothing specific. We discovered her association with Joey Juarez on the news along with the rest of the world. However, our informant continued to provide us with information regarding your welfare, as well as the children's."

"And you never asked me directly?"

"Though we appreciated the birth announcements, we assumed from their formality you shared Joanna's wish to have nothing to do with us."

Aubrey fidgeted. "I'm sorry."

"I sense this comes as a shock to you. The man we hired has been very discreet."

"At the least, I will let the children know they have loving grandparents. No need to stay in the shadows any longer."

Mrs. Curtis picked up a stack of photographs. "We have managed to observe the children from time to time. We saw Paul play at St. Andrews last year. And my husband gave the commencement address at Darlene's graduation from Georgetown, though she did not know her connection to him, of course. We'll be quite pleased to attend Bradley's wedding. I can't tell you how much this openness means to us. Now we can approach the children directly."

"That's why I'm here today, to confirm my note. I want you to be involved with your grandchildren from here on out."

The congressman shook Aubrey's hand. "Thank you."

Mrs. Curtis put the empty tea cups on the tray and rang for Rosa. "I hope you understand our desperate espionage and will find the grace to forgive us."

That might take him awhile. Though miffed, he understood why. "I have a friend who is a private detective. After Darlene's birth, Joanna disappeared for a long time. I asked him to find her. He did, and she came back. At that time, he discovered her connection to you. That's when I sent you Darlene's birth announcement. When Joanna returned, I tried to convince her to contact you. She threatened to divorce me. I never understood her resistance any more than you did. Like you, I respected her wishes. But, I did risk notifying you of both Paul and Bradley's births."

Mrs. Curtis smiled. "We may be stilted in our old-world atmosphere. Let me assure you, we are God-fearing people and believe in the power of prayer. We trusted you with our grandchildren, because we knew you were a highly principled man."

The words seemed empty, yet necessary. "I'm sorry for the lost years …"

Mrs. Curtis raised her free hand in polite interruption. "Let's not look to our regrets, which are many. We prefer to look forward."

Aubrey stood to leave, and the congressman walked with him to the door. He leaned in to whisper. "Sorry to hear this mess has landed you in a hot spot with your church. Is there anything we can do to help?"

"How did you know?" Stupid question. Whoever spied for them would have known. "My friend and I have rented an apartment in the city. We'll move in right after Thanksgiving. I have a small savings and should be fine for the time being until I find employment."

"Do you think you'll want to pastor a new church?"

Could he trust this man with the vision? "In a way. I'd like to start up a new work, much more in depth than my street ministry. An interfaith, intergovernmental rescue program for those trapped in the web of addiction. It's one thing to desire a change and quite another to leave the old life behind. The traditional church is ill-equipped to help the criminal element. With no hope for the future, most addicts return to the past."

Congressman Curtis nodded. "We'd like to help. Please keep us informed of your progress."

They shook hands as if old friends.

"One more thing, Aubrey. Say the word, and I can put an end to this media circus."

"You can do that?" Of course, he could. Congressman Curtis owned the ear of presidents, current and past. Perhaps the reason Joanna's link to Washington remained hidden from mainstream media.

"I'm saying the word."

"Consider it done."

CHAPTER 17

Joanna stared at the flecks of falling snow. Tomorrow would be Thanksgiving—her last. She wished she could spend the day with someone she loved—not in a budget motel. A year ago, she wouldn't have cared if she spent a holiday alone ... as long as she had her heroin to keep her company.

She mourned the missed opportunities and wondered what life might have been if only she'd given her life to God earlier instead of waiting until death's shadow hovered.

"Lucas, I haven't slept two nights in the same bed since the shooting. Can't we put a stop to all this moving around? Tomorrow is Thanksgiving."

"I know this hopscotch life has been difficult. I'd like you to have company. Unfortunately, there are too many risks. Maybe after I get your taped testimony and affidavits. There are still a few glitches yet."

She hoped Lucas might stay a little longer than his usual five-minute chat. Aside from his snide remarks, he brought news from the outside world—of Aubrey and the children.

"We'll get you a turkey dinner with all the trimmings from Home Foods Market. Casey will keep you company. He talks enough for ten people." Lucas's cell buzzed. "Skylar, here."

He cocked his head and stared at her—a fraction of a second. "I have to take this outside."

Was the call about her. If only it could have been for her.

Casey rose from his seat near the window. "Do you need anything, Miss Joanna?"

"No. I'm good. Tell me more about your family. Got any pictures?"

He pulled out his cell, brought up his photo gallery, and pulled a chair next to hers. "These first ones are from my granddaughter's first birthday party last month." He bragged on every child and grandchild. Then he clicked on to a video. The curly mopped toddler swiped her tray free of chocolate cake, frosting smeared across her face.

Something about the blonde-haired man standing in the corner rang familiar. "Casey, may I take a closer look. The sunlight blocked his features. She couldn't be certain. "Casey, who's this in the corner?"

"That's Dickey Jones, my son-in-law."

"Where does he work?"

"He's a pharmacist at Mercy Hospital."

"I thought I recognized him. He paid me a visit while I was there and mentioned a research project he's been involved with."

"Still is. He believes they're making great progress. He thinks that within twenty years, many cancers will be as treatable as the common cold. I wish it were now, Miss Joanna."

"I knew when I gave my heart to God, He did not intend to heal me physically."

"Are you absolutely sure?"

She squeezed Casey's hand. "I'm at peace. I am grateful for what he has given me through all of this … to see Aubrey one last time and know he has forgiven me. I'm ready whenever God wants me."

The door flew open followed by a gust of frigid air along with Gimbya, her nurse. She held up a box of frozen vanilla bars on a stick. "Best I could do, Miss Joanna."

She unwrapped the treat with gusto. "Yum. Thanks. I hope you didn't have to walk very far."

"Only a block." She headed back toward the door. "I'll be right back in."

Now what? Gimbya's care proved to be yet another blessing in this new world of chaos. More than a competent nurse, Gimbya had endeared herself to Joanna as a sister. Tall, with eyes like coconuts, she swayed with her movements as if performing an African fertility dance. She hummed songs in her ancestral language.

Though Casey loved to talk, Joanna appreciated the female companionship. Though she carried herself with all the regality of a queen, Gimbya served her patient with a servant's heart.

She came in with matching bed comforters. "I know the constant change in scenery is hard on you, Miss Joanna. At least, with these for decoration, each new room will have a sense of familiarity." The pattern was not what Joanna would have picked out. However, Gimbya's thoughtfulness more than made up for her taste.

"I wish I could have kept Big Blue."

"Big Blue?"

"A stuffed animal my husband had given me. I had to leave it behind at the nursing home. It's the only possession I had there besides my Bible that I miss."

Joanna took two bites of the vanilla ice-cream bar. Blasted nausea. "I'm sorry, Gimbya. I can't eat any more. I so appreciate everything you do. I wish I could do better for you."

She scowled. "Mr. Skylar's worried about your loss of appetite. I worry too. You're so skinny I can count your bones."

"You're a good nurse, Gimbya. I don't know what I would do without you. Since I'm not allowed computer access, Casey found out what your name means … Princess. Are you descended from royalty?"

She nodded. "Though the United States is my native country—my family has been here for three generations—to answer your question, yes, my great-great grandfather was a tribal chief."

The descendant of royals held Joanna's hand while she puked.

Her knees buckled. "I think I better get to bed."

Gimbya shooed Casey out of the room. "You give Miss Joanna her privacy while I help her get into her nightclothes."

He scooted outside like a kid sent to his room.

Gimbya took Joanna's soiled clothes and placed them into a bag. "I'll ask Mr. Skylar to be certain to land us in a hotel with a washing machine tomorrow. If not, maybe he'd let me shop for some more clothes for you."

Her nurse's taste in clothes ran along the same line as her taste in bedding. Yet, Joanna would wear whatever Gimbya picked out. Kindness never clashed with compassion.

Once Joanna was in bed, Gimbya handed her the plain black Bible Casey had given her. "Anything else you need, Miss Joanna?"

"Just girl company. Although, I suppose we shouldn't leave Casey in the cold for too long."

The women laughed, the reverberation like cymbals at the end of a symphony.

Gimbya opened the door and gestured for Casey to come back inside.

He shivered. "Next time give me enough warning to put my coat on. It's getting cold out there."

Joanna smiled. Gimbya and Casey jabbed one another like siblings at a dinner table, their banter a source of amusement.

"Gimbya, I'm curious. Where did you go to nursing school?"

"Columbia. I will return in the Spring to begin work on my Master's. When I'm finished, I hope to go to Africa. My church has a hospital mission program in Kenya where I can teach others."

"I'm glad you're here now." A pain shot across her abdomen. Gimbya scowled. "Time for your medicine. You should sleep now."

Joanna nodded, though she slept more hours in the day than an elderly cat. "Thank you again for the comforters." Joanna warmed with the thought, how the God of all Comfort had supplied her with angels—Casey, Gimbya, and even the crusty Roberts who went out of his way to keep his charge supplied with cinnamon sticks for her tea. Though she had everything she needed, she wearied of the constant guard—not a moment of privacy.

Not the first time in her life she'd been under constant surveillance. Her father had insisted on an army of bodyguards, and Joey's goons had followed her everywhere. She should be used to the routine by now.

Lucas came back in, again without knocking, his face frozen in contemplation. "Good news. The Grand Jury is scheduled for the first week in January."

"Five more weeks of this? I'm so lucky."

"I'm sorry it's not the Ritz. Believe it or not, you're safer in these roach motels. Nobody pays attention to what happens here—the fewer questions asked, the better off you are." He sighed as if to continue but stopped.

"What else?"

Lucas shrugged his shoulders. "You read me like a book."

"So?"

He glanced toward her watchdogs. "I need to talk to Miss Curtis alone."

Casey and Gimbya grabbed their coats and stepped outside. Lucas pulled up a chair next to Joanna's bed. She half expected him to hold her hands like a parent bringing bad news to their child. "It seems Casey's been talking to his know-it-all son-in-law. All on the up and up, of course—the boy wonder doesn't know it's you. He only knows that his father-in-law is concerned about a friend who is terminally ill. Casey told me about the research project Dickey's involved with. I did some research on the program."

Joanna yanked on the comforter. "I thought you agreed to let me live out my days in peace. I don't want any more chemo."

"It's not chemo in the traditional sense with an IV and tubes. Not your typical pill, either. It's palliative. More like a supplement. Not a cure."

"Why bother?"

"The medication slows the cancer, and reportedly gives the patient a few extra months as well as dulls the pain without the side effect of drowsiness. You'd have a much-improved quality of life."

"You call being a motel prisoner quality?"

"We'll have your statements, of course, but your testimony at the Grand Jury will weigh more. I'll announce to the world the gross error we made about your death. You'll be able to see Aubrey too. If he's crazy enough to take care of you, we'll arrange for hospice at his place."

"Don't lie to me, Lucas. You know as well as I do, I'll have to stay in witness protection until the end. I'll never see Aubrey again."

"You'd live long enough to put Joey behind bars, though. That's what you wanted, wasn't it?"

"I thought testifying would be the right thing to do. I'm not so sure anymore."

Pain tore through her chest. She gasped, drew a few deep breaths, then went on. "You think I should take this drug? What about side effects? There must be some."

Lucas hesitated. "I can't say for sure—the drug's too new. And … um … I'd have to break a few regs to get you into the program."

"Never knew you to care about rules before, Lucas. So, are these rules you'll break worse than faking my death?"

"Ouch. To coin an old phrase, 'Where there's a will, there's a way.' As for side effects? Dickey says the patient feels slightly sicker for a few days, then gradually improves. Most patients experience a sense of euphoria."

"And the worst scenario?"

"The pill won't kill you."

"The cancer will, though."

Lucas strode to the other side of the room. "I'm not completely without compassion, you know. If there's something out there to help you that won't compromise your testimony, I'd say we should let you try it."

"All I want is for this to be over. I'd like to die in peace."

Lucas walked to the window, perhaps to avoid direct eye contact. "You won't survive until January without something. We've got nothing to lose."

Nothing for me to lose—everything for you to gain. "Fine. I'll take the pill."

CHAPTER 18

Gregg Fischer gazed at the ID on the in-coming call. Congressman Curtis. He picked up the phone, answered the cell's chime, and examined the plush leather chair delivered to his office earlier in the day. "Thanks for the heads up, Congressman, and for not blowing the whistle on me with Beaumont."

He swallowed a bite of his roast beef sandwich while the congressman talked.

"Mr. Fischer, I wanted you to know your services are no longer needed."

The gravy train had to stop sometime. "Totally understood. Glad Aubrey has opened the door to communication with your grandchildren. I think that's wonderful. I do owe you a debt of gratitude for this job you helped me get, so, if there's anything I can do for you in the future, please let me know."

"I assume you like sports?"

"Big Redskins fan."

"Redskins? I'd have pegged you a Patriots devotee."

"Beaumont is. He lived his whole life in Vermont before coming to the DC area. I'm originally from New York City, but I've always rooted for the Redskins."

Congressman Curtis laughed. "How did you and Aubrey become such great pals?"

"My parents moved to Brattleboro when I was in the eighth grade. Beaumont took me under his wing. I guess he was into projects back then too."

"I'll see if I can obtain season tickets for next year."

"Not necessary. But I won't turn them down."

Nice to have friends in high places. Gregg disconnected and took another bite as he mused over Beaumont's probable discomfort when he discovered the congressman had him and the kids tailed. If people knew how easily powerful people could gain private information, perhaps more would pay attention to the details of their everyday lives. Then again, perhaps the delusion of privacy is an entitlement of a free society.

Regret clawed at Gregg's conscience. He hated to keep his connection to Congressman Curtis a secret. Didn't matter that the congressman had reached out to Gregg with an offer far greater than a poor boy could imagine. He'd turned down the initial offer. The congressman proved to be insistent, each offer more lucrative than the previous one. He'd finally rationalized that if he didn't accept, Congressman Curtis would take his gold elsewhere. Better Beaumont be spied on by a friend as opposed to a stranger. At least this way, Gregg could control what leaked.

The rewards were endless, especially this job with a nice office and antique desk.

Joanna sure gave up the life of Riley when she ran away after her breakup with Skylar. Gregg mulled on her tragic life. More to be pitied than hated. She had everything to live for—powerful, yet loving parents, beauty, smarts, and a husband willing to die for her. Yet, she threw everything away for junk. Drug addicts selfishly inflicted havoc on the innocent … like the thief who took Marla from him.

He'd have mused all day if not for the sudden shock of his coat being thrown in his face. Jacobs, his office partner, laughed. "Time to go home, Fischer. Enjoy the holiday."

He rose and disentangled himself from his London Fog trench coat. How cliché. Still, a look he preferred. Not for the status. More for comfort, gumshoe that he was. "You got foam on those soles, Jacobs? Never heard you come in."

He'd worked alone since he first put out his shingle. However, with pay this good, he'd learn to work alongside an intellectual dwarf if necessary.

Gregg handed Jacobs the pile of photos he'd put on the desk. "I glanced at these. Looks like you've got the doc nailed. Enough evidence for our client to go to the cops, I'd say. Only, looks like he was in cahoots with someone. I suppose we should try to find out who before we turn him in. Too bad for the doc. Seems like a nice guy. Wonder why he scammed the company?"

Jacobs shrugged. "People will do most anything if the price is right. You going to Brattleboro for Thanksgiving or staying in the city?"

He'd like to see Jason. However, an afternoon with Marla's parents was out of the question. Maybe he could manage to swallow his pride during Christmas for his son's sake. As far as Gregg knew the kid planned to be with his grandparents as always. "We—Beaumont and me—are having company."

Jacobs leaned forward, his whiskey-tainted breath nauseatingly close. "Company—as in female?"

Gregg nodded.

"Your girl or Beaumont's?"

"Neither. More like a mutual friend. I've thought about asking her out. Can't muster the nerve."

Jacobs jabbed Gregg with a bony finger. "Kind of hard to believe you'd back off from any woman."

"The situation is complicated."

Jacobs stroked his goatee. "Not much about life that isn't."

They exited together. "I suppose you're right. Happy Thanksgiving, Fischer." When they reached the parking lot, Jacobs went toward his Porsche and Gregg for his rented SUV. He should probably buy a new car rather than bring his Lexus down from Vermont.

The rental's purr matched the grumblings of growing self-incrimination. He should come clean with Beaumont. How? When? One didn't begin a conversation with, "I've made the bulk of my income spying on you."

And what of Cynthia? If he didn't take the plunge soon, he might never know where their relationship could lead.

Tomorrow. Tomorrow would be soon enough.

CHAPTER 19

Aubrey passed the turkey platter for its second round. No small task to vacate a position, find an affordable place to live, and set up a new ministry. He'd have one more Thanksgiving in the parsonage before the move tomorrow. Despite enormous loss, there was much to celebrate.

Cynthia took another slice of turkey. "Thanks for the invitation, Aubrey. Everything is lovely. Gregg said you were a good cook."

"I know how to cook. Just don't like to very much. The family's growing. Maybe the time has come to reinstitute Sunday Dinner."

Percy buttered another slice of bread. "Ain't one fer fancy cookin', but I sure do like this bread." He shook his head for emphasis. "Yes, siree! Mighty good eats, Pastor Aubrey."

No more sermons to prepare for the immediate future. Would he be anyone's pastor ever again?

Cynthia's eyes danced. Aubrey hated the conflict within. Why couldn't he attempt a relationship with her beyond friendship? Maybe if they'd met before he married Joanna? No point in maybes. Joanna possessed him as much in death as she had in life. Though he could not push her from his mind, he would not dwell on his loss. Thanksgiving was a time for gratitude. He determined to refocus on his many blessings—chief of which was Bradley's wedding.

He and Trish complimented one another. Where Bradley tended toward morose quietness, Trish infused the air with vivaciousness. She possessed the same dry wit as Joanna. Fortunately for Bradley, Trish's faith defined her as much as her charm.

If only I'd married a believer.

He rebuked the thought. He'd sensed more than God's permission to marry Joanna. Rather, he was convinced the Lord had nudged him in her direction. He thought of the biblical Hosea. God sometimes ordained marriage outside the bonds of common sense. Her pregnancy had done little to change his mind. But, would he still have proposed if he'd known about her addiction? Probably.

He remembered the moment he first saw her. She sat alone, an ethereal vision as she drank cinnamon tea. He knew in that instant he'd marry her, before he even knew her name. If he could have changed one thing about his life, he'd have hoped for a different end. Still, God's power reached beyond death, and he rested in the hope the Lord might yet answer Joanna's prayer for purpose.

"Great dinner, Dad." Bradley offered a congratulatory slap on the back, then passed the platter to Paul. "Darlene doesn't know what she's missing."

Paul forked two large pieces and plunked them on his plate. "Any more gravy?"

Trish passed the boat across the table. "Thanks for making the gravy, Cynthia. Aubrey's a great cook, except for his gravy. It's always lumpy. Yours was delicious."

Cynthia acknowledged the compliment with a wave of her coffee cup.

Turkey, potatoes, cranberry sauce, corn, squash, dressing, and rolls made a third relay around the table. Aubrey savored each minute of the mundane that surrounded him. Joy could indeed surpass grief. "I still can't get over how well Bradley carved the turkey."

"No sweat, Dad."

"You do know that carving meat is the man's job."

Trish and Cynthia scowled like twins, and Bradley laughed. "Yeah. Right, Dad. I think probably culinary arts are a little lower on the list of marriage priorities. Paul's the one who needs to learn a few domestic skills. Doesn't even do his own laundry."

Paul raised his head. "Why should I when I can afford to hire it done?"

"There he goes again. Bragging on his money."

"You didn't mind my wedding present."

"Who'd refuse a Caribbean cruise?" Bradley buttered a roll. "Seriously, though, it's a nice gift."

Trish reached across the narrow table and clasped Paul's hand. "I'm glad you'll be Bradley's best man. The sentiment means so much to him."

Bradley planted a kiss on Trish's cheek. "Didn't I tell you this is the greatest woman in the world?"

Paul gave Bradley an elbow jab. "I should warn you, Trish. Bradley snores."

"I do not!"

"Do too."

"Okay, boys. Quite enough." Aubrey grabbed the boys' collars in playful mockery. "Stop, right now, or I'll send you both to your rooms."

Cackles from all sides of the table echoed from the ceiling, except for Fischer who'd been pensive all through dinner. He'd pushed his turkey around his plate like a child who spurns spinach. Cynthia apparently noticed as well. "You've been quiet today, Gregg. What's wrong?"

He stared at his plate. "I'm a little tired is all. Jacobs and I have been working hard on a new case. Pharmacy fraud."

Bradley passed the gravy boat to Fischer. "Try Cynthia's gravy. It's guaranteed lump-free."

Fischer spooned a generous amount onto his potatoes. "Sorry. I didn't mean to bring the party down."

Cynthia glanced around the dining room. "Such a beautiful parsonage. Although, I expect with Darlene's help, your new apartment will look very nice. Too bad she couldn't be with us today."

Bradley frowned. "She's the worst workaholic I ever knew."

Aubrey sighed. Though adults, he still found himself in the middle of his children's sibling rivalry. "Now Bradley—"

"It's a disease, Dad. She needs serious help. Remember how she worked five days straight on the Tolland brief? Didn't stop to eat or sleep and ended up in the hospital from exhaustion."

"Sis knows her own mind. If she prefers to eat a grocery store takeout over a home-cooked meal, we'll love her anyway."

Cynthia pushed her plate slightly forward "Well, I for one can't eat another bite. May I help clear the table, Aubrey?"

Fischer stacked the plates. "Beaumont cooks, and I do the cleanup. I'd appreciate the help, though. Why don't the rest of you go into the den and watch the game."

Cynthia picked up a tray of plates. "Trish and I could manage, Gregg, if you wanted to watch the game with the men. I'd like to hear her wedding plans."

"Let Trish spend the extra time with Bradley. I don't mind missing some of the game. Besides, there's a question I want to ask you."

Cynthia had anticipated the question as she grabbed a dishtowel. Gregg loaded the dishwasher and scrubbed the pots and pans.

About time, Gregg Fischer.

So why did she tingle like a young girl who was about to be asked to the prom? Her cheeks heated as he tugged on the dish towel, his smile like an impish boy's. He braced himself against the sink.

Here it is.

"I'm clumsy at this, Cynthia."

"Spit it out and we'll deal with the aftermath."

"What's between you and Beaumont … now that Joanna's no longer in the way?"

You're right. This is very awkward, Gregg Fischer. She squelched the urge to smack him across the face.

"I sense you didn't like the way I posed that question?"

"On that score, you figured correctly."

"I told you I'm no good at this."

"And I told you already that we're friends. You think I'm in love with Aubrey?"

Gregg nodded.

She threw her dish towel into the drainer, grabbed him by both shoulders, and spun him around. "I admire Aubrey very much. At some point, perhaps, I was even infatuated. Never love. And certainly, not now. How could I be when I'm interested in someone else?"

"Yeah?"

"Look me in the eyes, Gregg Fischer. You might not have the eloquence of a politician, but you're a good judge of whether someone's telling the truth. There never has been, nor will there ever be, anything more than friendship between Aubrey and me."

He pulled her into a firm embrace—his kiss left no doubts as to his desire.

CHAPTER 20

Gregg yawned. What a whirlwind of activity within two weeks—the move into the apartment he'd share with Beaumont and dates with Cynthia nearly every night. Now, Beaumont had roped Gregg into helping with renovations to the ministry headquarters, a tenement that should have been torn down years ago.

Friendship required he help whether he agreed with the programs Beaumont envisioned or not. Nor could he say no to the congressman, who worked tirelessly beside Beaumont to get the ministry up and running.

No one else could have worked through the myriad entrapments of red tape as quickly as Congressman Curtis. Most likely he'd made a call or two to Brigg's higher ups, the reason the detective agency insisted their newest employee become more civic-minded.

The best motivator for involvement with this project was more time with Cynthia, who believed in the ministry as much as Beaumont.

He gazed the circumference of the main floor and shook his head at the amount of work yet to be done. Beaumont was more anxious to hit the sidewalks. Congressman Curtis felt appearances were important. He was right about one thing. A good scrubbing and a few coats of paint would make the place more attractive to benefactors, which was the reason he put up the money needed for renovations and insisted the materials should be of the highest quality. In this, all agreed. The reclamation of a building most considered worth the expense of demolition symbolized the core of Aubrey's mission. Perhaps why he didn't want to hire the work done.

Gregg grabbed the paintbrush from Cynthia's hands and stepped back to examine her work. "A little more practice and you can sign up as a carpenter's helper."

"Is that a compliment or an insult?"

A resistant blob of paint on Cynthia's lower lip begged attention. He wiped it off and pulled her in for a kiss.

She shoved him away. "You're incorrigible."

"And you're incredible." A weak sentiment when he wanted to shout from the roof how much he loved her. The words formed in his heart, yet he still feared to speak them.

Beaumont shook his head. "Okay, you two. Later. I'd like to finish this floor by nightfall. Fischer, why don't you tackle the back where the prayer room will be."

Gregg scanned the large open area where Beaumont stood. "What will you use this space for?"

"Probably for an activity room. Sports Gallery has agreed to donate a dart board and a Ping-Pong table."

Gregg snorted. "Aren't most hookers women?"

Cynthia punched his side. "Lots of women like to play Ping-Pong and darts. I know I do."

Gregg gave her a quick peck on the lips. "You're not like most girls."

Beaumont pointed toward the far end of the room. "We'll put a television in the corner over there. Jonas donated a DVD player and a ton of movies … mostly classics. Second Chances thrift store has donated boxes of books for a library. Literacy Volunteers will send helpers to improve our clients' reading skills. The Unemployment Bureau wants to provide job skills training. If all goes well, this will be the center for our rehabilitation services."

Cynthia smiled. "Amazing what you've accomplished already, Aubrey." She glanced around the room. "Look how you've redeemed this old house."

Beaumont nearly jumped off the ladder. "That's it."

Gregg shook from doubt. All this money invested for what? Most of those who'd come for help would be back on the street within a month. "What's it?"

"I have a pile of paperwork to go through, and I needed a name for the ministry. Redemption's Corner. What do you think?" He flashed the first genuine smile since Joanna died.

"Perfect." Cynthia stroked the doorframe. "I think we're looking at the original woodwork. I'd say this house was constructed a few decades before the Civil War. The rest of the neighborhood seems younger as if built around this house. Shame such a valuable historic district has been allowed to deteriorate into a slum."

Beaumont stiffened as if with pride. "Rumor has it Abe Lincoln often visited the original owner."

Gregg laughed. "What home in an historical area doesn't lay claim to hosting a former, beloved president? Jacobs says this used to be a swanky neighborhood until drug traffickers took over."

Beaumont's face paled. Probably no accident he chose this area for the ministry—smack dab in the middle of Juarez territory. What better way to plan revenge for Joanna's death than to convert her murderer's gang members?

Gregg rubbed his stomach. "When's Jonas coming back with those subs? I'm starved."

Beaumont shrugged his shoulders. "It's been over an hour since he left. Should be here any time."

"I'll get started in the back room. Dibs on the ladder."

He brought the ladder into the back and returned to the common room for fresh paint just as Cynthia popped open a new can, then gazed at Aubrey. "I like Jonas," she said. "In fact, I think you've strung together a pretty good executive board. Including Darlene, I understand."

"Only for legal advice." Beaumont picked up a rag off the pine desk donated by the Salvation Army. "I think I'll start cleaning the windows."

Gregg carried paint supplies toward the back. "I can handle this room on my own. Cynthia, why don't you help Beaumont in here?"

She threw him a surprised look. "Okay."

Gregg laughed. "Don't get so occupied you forget to tell me when lunch arrives."

Cynthia grabbed another rag, reluctant to leave Gregg. How she adored him. She hoped he loved her as deeply as she loved him. Though he didn't say the words, she sensed he did.

Aubrey seemed uncomfortably intent on the task at hand. Should she interrupt his thoughts? Funny how much she cared about this new venture of his. Should she set up permanent residence in the area? Dad agreed to a quit claim, and now she was part owner of his house. So, she had a place to stay when he went into the nursing home. The social worker expected an opening soon. She'd already asked for early retirement. Why not have her belongings from Chicago sent to Silver Spring?

Aubrey's ministry would be a good retirement job for her. She'd volunteered to help with the first clothing drive. Gregg said he'd serve as a trustee, though she suspected he was more motivated by friendship with the ministry's founder than a deep desire to affect change in a prostitute's life. Or perhaps he volunteered because of her insistence he be involved. Maybe she shouldn't have nagged him. Men disliked being dictated to. At least Donald did. He'd disappear for hours if she repeated a request more than two times in an hour.

How her thoughts rambled. She turned her attention to the mildew-encased windows. "Aubrey, these should be replaced. I think they're beyond help."

He dropped the rag. "You're right. I'll put that on the list. Doesn't mean we can't begin a few projects by next week. We would never be this far along without the congressman's generosity."

"And influence. I'm amazed at the red-tape he's been able to circumvent."

Aubrey nodded.

"Have you named a coordinating board yet?"

"Congressman Curtis suggested we have a blend of community organizations, as well as interfaith leaders. So far there's Devon O'Brien, the Catholic priest, Jorge Gonzales from the Salvation Army, Brian Wong from Social Services, and Francine Holloway from Narcotics Anonymous. We should have the rest of the board in place by early next week. I'm excited about the wrap-around approach."

"Wrap around?"

"Where agencies combine services in a team approach to problem solving."

"Sounds wonderful. I would suspect the drug addict's problems are multi-faceted."

Loud footsteps echoed from the stairwell. "Hopefully, that's Jonas with our subs."

Cynthia motioned Aubrey to stay put. "I'll meet him in the hall. He probably has his hands full."

She should have known better than to walk forward and look back at the same time. She tripped on the paint can. "Oh, dear," she said as she fell into a pool of golden liquid. Aubrey helped her to stand. He grabbed a clean rag and wiped the paint off her hands—just as Jonas knocked on the door and Gregg came in from the back room.

"I smell subs!" He stopped short as he glanced back and forth between Cynthia's giggles and Aubrey's grunt laughs. "What's going on here?"

CHAPTER 21

Joanna smiled as Casey tipped his cap. "Glad to see you up and about today, Miss Joanna."

She'd like to hug the big bear of a man but doubted her arms would stretch around his middle. "I was beginning to think the pills would kill me before the cancer did. I hadn't been this sick since my pregnancies. I feel much better today." Though the improvement would only be temporary, she welcomed the boost in strength.

Casey pulled back the window curtain. "Glad Dickey found a way to get you into his program."

Probably for the best Casey didn't know his son-in-law had connived a way for her to get into the trials. And that Lucas most likely made a deal with the devil to arrange her admission. The less she knew the better. Sometimes, ignorance was indeed bliss. "Casey, is it still raining? I thought I saw a few flecks of snow in the air."

"It's a lot warmer than when we checked the weather report this morning." Casey shuffled his feet the way he did when not sure if he should divulge something or not. "I thought you'd want to know. Mr. Skylar's stopping by this morning. Says he has news."

"Something to do with the case, I suspect. I have no idea what's going on in the real world. Lucas won't let me watch the news on television. I'm not even supposed to read a newspaper."

Casey laughed. "Is that why every morning you ask me who's President?" He handed her the cartoon section of The Washington Post. "Maybe you'd like to do the crossword puzzle today?"

"Maybe later."

Casey glanced out the window. "Mr. Skylar's here."

Lucas's knock seemed impossibly more aggressive than ever.

"Come in."

He nodded at Casey. "Leave us."

Lucas paced as he searched the room and picked up the section of paper Casey had left on Joanna's bedside table. "What's this?

"Just the crossword puzzle, Lucas. I've been a good girl and have obeyed your orders explicitly. Casey fills me in on world events. No harm in a little diversion.

"I guess not. Where's Gimbya?"

Joanna thought Lucas the most arrogant man on the face of the earth until she remembered she once loved him. "She's shopping. I'd like a few changes of clothes that don't hang on me like a scarecrow's costume."

"Understandable."

"I'm sure you didn't come all the way over here to check up on my nurse. Casey said you had news."

He paced again, worry in each step. "It seems your husband has not given up his desire to save every hooker and junkie in Washington." He yanked the paper from his inside coat pocket and rustled it open to the religious news. With a disgusted shrug, he showed her Aubrey's picture next to the story about a ministry he and her father had begun, Redemption's Corner.

Why must Aubrey see himself as the savior of all mankind? That was the Lord's job, and God didn't need the paltry efforts of a sincere but misguided martyr. She gazed up at Lucas. "Redemption's Corner is in the middle of Joey's territory."

"You married an idiot, Joanna. He's going to get himself killed."

"Since when do you care what happens to a man you called an insignificant preacher?"

His pace quickened. "Stirring up Juarez's territory is going to blow this case. I feel it."

"It's the case you're worried about? Nothing more?"

Lucas swiped his hair, a slight tremor in his hand. "Maybe I have a heart after all. I'm worried for Darlene's sake. I can't be a part of her life, and Beaumont is the only father she's ever known. I'd hate for something to happen to him."

"Why the sudden fatherly interest? You've never met her."

He turned toward the window.

"Or have you?"

"She doesn't know who I am. One of her clients is up for manslaughter. While at court, I overheard her conversation with the prosecutor on a possible deal and couldn't resist the opportunity. I stuck my head in on pretense. She does look like me, doesn't she?"

"You whisked me away before I was able to see any of the children. Aubrey showed me pictures. Yes, she does resemble you."

Without warning, Lucas moved to Joanna's side and gently cupped her chin in his hand. "I think she favors her mother more."

Lucas held her hand as he spoke, his tone tender—tender for him, at least. "I know I acted selfishly back then. Rash and impulsive. I did love you, though. You should have told me you decided to go through with the pregnancy. I'd have helped raise her. I'm not that much of a cad. You never gave me the chance to be a father to her."

Did he truly care about his daughter, or was he using Darlene to manipulate his witness? "Be part of her life now, Lucas. You need each other."

"When the time's right, I'll tell her who I am. She has enough drama to deal with for now. Apparently, Beaumont has acquainted your children with their famous grandparents."

"What do you mean?"

Lucas stood, and the corners of his lips formed a sneer. "The noble Reverend Beaumont made a visit to your folks and invited them to your son's wedding."

"That's why my father has helped Aubrey with his ministry?"

"Not just personally. He's proposed legislation to make government funds available to faith-based initiatives that help addicts and prostitutes turn their lives around. A lot of Congressman Curtis's peers are behind the concept of an interagency approach to combat this problem. Beaumont's program will include law enforcement, places of worship, and human services agencies. The Congressman hopes Redemption's Corner will be a model for future non-profits in the area."

Joanna instantly filled with worry. If Lucas's information was correct, her father's life was now as much at risk as Aubrey's.

"And you know this, how?"

"I make it my business to know the business of others, especially where you are concerned. A conviction against Juarez is my ticket to a political career. I don't want anything to compromise a victory."

Her heart burned with animosity. "So, you're more worried about your precious case than Aubrey, your daughter, or my parents."

"I do care. Perhaps I've been more focused on this case than I should be. I won't pretend. I'm a selfish man. You know that more than anyone."

"I pity you."

Aubrey had always questioned why she ran away from parents who obviously loved her. She'd hated the notoriety, the constant thief of privacy. When her children were born, she'd hoped to spare them from the constant publicity. She'd worried they, too, would become political pawns for her parents' enemies. Foolishness. In the end, instead of protection, her decision had robbed them of their heritage.

Shame filled her as she remembered the scene when Aubrey took her to rehab after Darlene was born. She'd flown into a rage at his confession he'd sent her parents a birth announcement. She claimed they were as caring as machines. Faith helps one see the world through a kinder set of glasses. She remembered them now for who they truly were—imperfect people whose only sin was that they smothered her with love and protection. Her child's heart longed to be cradled once more in her mother's arms.

Lucas walked to the door. "I need to get back." His hand rested on the knob. "Your judgment of me is not only harsh, it's unfounded. I do care—more than you realize."

This time, the door closed softly.

CHAPTER 22

These weeks with Gregg had been more than wonderful—a cyclone of excitement as they unraveled the complex layers of each other's personality. But the last couple of days, she'd noticed a marked increase in his moodiness, unresponsive to her attempts to pull him from his pensive pit.

They'd been to museums, restaurants, walked the beach, and circled the Reflecting Pool. Today, they played golf, undaunted by the forty-degree temperatures. They both had moved from cold climates where spring golf sometimes required mittens and a knit hat. To play a few days before Christmas was a treat beyond belief.

Perhaps Gregg's old-school gallantry drew her to him. He hung up her coat, opened doors for her, and walked on the traffic side of the street. Though independent since the day her father walked out, she enjoyed the layers of protectiveness.

Gregg sat next to her on the couch, lifted her hair and kissed her on the neck. She knew he loved her. Yet, she longed to hear him say so.

He whispered in her ear as he kissed her with more passion than might be wise this early in their relationship. "I think you should buy the pizza."

Perhaps this side of him topped the list of his many charms—to converse about the mundane through the heights of his passion. Something she found difficult to do, especially now. She breathed a response, "Why is that?"

"You never would have beaten me if my putt on eighteen hadn't rimmed the hole and spun down the incline off the green. That cost me two strokes. Lucky for you—bad break for me." He pulled her impossibly closer. Her heart skipped more than a few beats. Any more heat in his kisses, she'd have to call the paramedics.

She inched closer. "A deal's … a deal, Gregg. I won. You lost. You're buying … you cheapskate."

He leaned against the couch and stroked his chin where stubble sprouted like spots on a potato. "Do you want to order in? I bought your favorite movie while out this morning."

"Gone with the Wind?"

"No. I thought it was Casablanca."

Close. At least he figured out the kind of movies she liked. "My second favorite."

He slid from the couch to a stand. "I'll be right back. Papa John's number is on the refrigerator. Beaumont and I order from there quite often."

"It's not on your cell?"

"Beaumont usually does the ordering, and the number's on the fridge."

"Where is Aubrey today?"

"First meeting of the executive board."

"He's so eager to start the mission."

Gregg scowled as he pulled out his cell. "I'll put Papa John's number in my phone, so I don't have to leave you next time to place an order."

"Can't pull the number up on your phone?"

"It will be faster if I check the fridge."

She squeezed his hand. "Hurry back."

He kissed her again, then went into the kitchen.

At least for today, he seemed in better spirits. What caused his dark side to rear? Work?

She glanced around the apartment. This had been the first time she'd seen Aubrey and Gregg's new digs since they moved. Thanks to Darlene's help, the décor mixed the sensibilities of two diverse sensitivities. Oddly, the dichotomy worked. Aubrey's art and Gregg's sport posters. Gregg said he could appreciate art, and both he and Aubrey loved sports.

The apartment, perhaps, symbolized the whole of their friendship. That they'd maintained their bond for so many years baffled the mind. Like the characters from The Odd Couple, their personalities clashed at every turn—Aubrey more like Felix, with the exception of his love of sports, and Gregg was an Oscar, though he'd become distraught if his chili didn't taste quite right.

Gregg dove onto the couch. "There, your highness. Your dinner has been ordered exactly to your specifications—sausage, mushrooms, and extra cheese. Now, where were we?" No memory problem. He found her lips with no trouble.

Gregg pleasured in calling her by royal nicknames. Normally, she detested pet names between romantic partners. Yet, the unpretentious way he used them only drew her to him like taffy—the man a delicious mixture of chauvinism and tenderness. Genuineness … that's what made her love

Gregg Fischer. He wore his emotions—all of them—whether in a dour state of mind or ecstatic to be in her presence … like now.

"If that pizza doesn't get here soon, I could forget about eating for the next few hours. What about you?"

"Hold your horses, Mr. Fischer. I'm not ready for that big step, yet. Though I'd be a liar if I said the idea hadn't crossed my mind."

He leaned back against the couch. "I'll wait until you're ready."

He still had not said the word love. Perhaps the thought scared him. Maybe she should cool things down a bit before they took their desire for one another too far and too soon—before she was sure of his love for her. She slid her palm over the leather sofa. "How nice of Congressman Curtis to send this over. He's been so kind lately—to both of you."

His cheeks turned scarlet.

"What did I say? If your face were any redder you'd be spouting steam like a cartoon character."

"It's nothing."

"Don't you like the couch?"

"Furniture is furniture. This suits Beaumont. At least I don't have to sit on the floor."

Time to dig deep. She'd either push Gregg away or find out what bothered him. "Out with it, Fischer. Something about this stuff sticks in your craw."

He rose with a start and went to the window. Was his worry so pervasive he couldn't even look at her? Only five minutes ago, he was ready to take her into his bedroom if she'd given him permission. What killed the mood?

"You'll despise me."

"I won't despise you, Gregg. Educators learn how to size people up in a short time. You're a good man. What could you have possibly done to make me feel differently towards you?"

"I love you, Cynthia. I think I've loved you from the moment I first saw you. Maybe I fell in love with you while I helped Aubrey find you. I know more about you than I knew about my wife. When I couldn't sleep, I'd reread your dossier. You are an amazing woman, Cynthia Prescott. And I don't deserve your affection."

Had he proclaimed his love for her only to end their relationship? "I love you, too, Gregg. So, what's the problem?"

He turned, his face taut. "The problem is, I don't believe you really do love me."

"Why would you think that?"

"Because I'm afraid you've fallen in love with the man I've pretended to be."

Cynthia gasped. "What are you saying?"

"I've kept a huge secret from Beaumont and from you. Once I returned to faith, I knew I needed to come clean. I've been too afraid."

"Afraid of what?"

"That, if I do, I'll lose you."

Secrets … why must people persist in them? Why couldn't human beings simply trust one another with truth? She gazed into his eyes. Was the fear she saw his or a reflection of her own? "Gregg, you're a good man— and a good friend to Aubrey."

"That's the problem. Everyone thinks I've done right by Beaumont over the years. Truth is, I haven't. Not for a long time."

Every instinct told her Gregg Fischer was an honorable man. Not a perfect man. One motivated by a good heart. "I know you never liked his wife."

Alarm filled her with Gregg's snarl. "True. I wept no tears for her when she died. That's not the issue."

"Then what?"

"Do you know why Beaumont is so tight with our dear Congressman Curtis?"

Was there a connection besides the ministry? "Aubrey's the amiable type. I assumed they knew each other from some other time."

"You might say so. Congressman Curtis is his father-in-law."

There was more to come, and Cynthia struggled to breathe as fear surged. Gregg's slow train to revelation could only mean the end of what had been love's sweet promise.

"And the children never knew?"

"They found out only recently. It's a long story."

"Better get started then."

He walked the room like an actor struts on stage, his body rigid. "When Joanna refused to tell Beaumont about her parents, he asked me to investigate her past. I had recently returned from military service and started my career as a private detective. No one was any more surprised to learn of her connection to one of Washington's most influential players than I was. Beaumont confronted Joanna after Darlene was born, but she insisted her parents must never be contacted. Beaumont respected her wishes, though he never understood why she felt as strongly as she did. He sent the congressman birth announcements with the explanation Joanna did not want the children contacted. I guess he thought a few postcards would satisfy Joanna's parents."

Cynthia's heart raced. Somehow, there was much more to this story. "Go on. I take it Congressman Curtis wasn't satisfied as Aubrey thought."

"In his letter to Congressman Curtis, Beaumont let it be known he'd discovered their connection through a friend of his who was a private investigator. Before long, the congressman hired me to keep him better informed about Beaumont and the children."

When Gregg finally faced her, tears filled his eyes. Guilt? That the congressman had hired him was not in and of itself a horrible thing. Quite understandable. Something else must have happened.

"Let me guess. He paid very well."

"Handsomely. Plenty of favors, too. Like my job with Briggs."

"And Aubrey had no idea?"

"I found out a lot about Joanna that I never shared with Beaumont … or Congressman Curtis. I deluded myself that the less Beaumont knew about where Joanna was, the better off he'd be. I did tell him I thought she might be in DC, but I never dreamed he'd quit his job and move to the area, though I did my best to persuade him not to try to find her."

"And the congressman? You never shared your knowledge about Joanna with him?"

"Why cause the man pain? He'd only hired me to keep him informed about the grandchildren. We'd made no other deal."

"Aubrey should have been told."

"I suppose. I found Joanna once. She begged me to keep silent. So, I felt justified."

"After she was killed, Beaumont visited her parents. He felt the time had come for the children to become acquainted with their grandparents. Congressman Curtis told Beaumont about hiring someone to stay informed regarding Joanna's family. However, the congressman didn't tell Beaumont I was the informant."

Though understandable, the years of deceit seemed unreasonable. They were friends.

"See, I can't help but wonder if I'd told Beaumont the truth from the onset, things might have been different for everyone. If Beaumont knew how deeply Joanna's parents cared, maybe he could have broken through her resistance, helped her, though she'd gone through more rehab sessions than a celebrity."

"Why did you keep Aubrey in the dark?"

Gregg turned away again. Cynthia held her breath. Why couldn't he face her? Perhaps she knew that answer, and the truth would tear them apart. "Because of the money?"

He nodded. Greed. The flaw in the man she could not overlook. "You're right. You're not the man I thought you were."

Gregg pounded the end table. He lowered his head, his breaths short and heated. "I knew you'd take his side in all this."

"I'm on no one's side. Only I can't comprehend how a friend could have kept up a ruse of that magnitude for so long."

"I won't defend myself. Lies between friends are never justified. I was wrong, and I'll bear the guilt to my dying day. What angers me most is I can see you're still in love with Beaumont. Aren't you? Why else would you care so deeply?"

Gregg raked his hair. She'd defended Beaumont, not her boyfriend. Her stated disappointment in him only solidified his suspicion. She'd dated him because Gregg Fischer was the alternative to Aubrey Beaumont—like someone prefers steak and settles for spaghetti because it's the only choice available. After a while, you get used to the spaghetti and don't hope for steak any more.

Gregg Fischer didn't want to be the spaghetti in Cynthia Prescott's life. Uncertainty pierced him. Better to lose her now than be torn to pieces later. Could he let her go without destroying himself in the process?

She gazed at him as if he were something not real.

The depths of his anger surprised him. He ranted accusations at her until Cynthia's look of horror clued him he'd crossed a line. Acid gurgled in his stomach. Jealousy consumed him. "I saw the two of you the day we painted Beaumont's offices."

Why did she continue to feign surprise? *Loyal to the bitter end, aren't you, sweetheart.* "Admit it, it's Beaumont you love. You're with me because I'm all you've got." He grabbed her arms and shook her. "Admit it."

She pushed free of his grasp. "Of course, I love Aubrey. As a dear friend. Not the same way I love you."

He pushed the coat rack to the floor. "If you weren't with me, you'd be with him."

"I can't convince someone of the truth who wants to believe a lie as badly as you do." She picked up her coat from the floor. "Goodbye, Gregg."

As the door closed, the beast already unloosed had free rein.

CHAPTER 23

Aubrey's thoughts flitted from one thing to the next on the long walk from the subway to the apartment. The brisk morning air invigorated his senses. He much preferred public transportation than driving, one advantage of living in DC rather than the suburbs. With Mrs. Curtis's help, he and Fischer had found an apartment close to mission headquarters. Not the best of neighborhoods, but outside of Juarez territory. Probably better for the children's sake when they visited and for Fischer.

As a pastor in Silver Spring, Aubrey's days were filled with study, prayer, calls on the sick and homebound, and meetings of some type or another. He'd spend a few hours each day in his office where he edited his sermons and chatted with other staff. His nights were crowded with church events where his attendance was expected … more like demanded. After long and busy days, gratitude filled him when his head reached the pillow at night.

He'd preached his first sermon today as Pastor Aubrey of Redemption's Corner. His congregants numbered about three dozen and consisted of prostitutes, pimps, alcoholics, drug addicts, and the occasional cop. His sanctuary was Mickey's Bar and Grille, given over Sunday afternoon for a hefty fee. Most of his parishioners began their day when the sun was at its highest.

After his sermon, he'd spent the early evening in Father O'Brien's church and handed out grocery bags to the homeless. As evening fell, he joined his ministry team who began their work when night covered the filth of human degradation, and street lamps offered a slight legitimacy to the uninformed. The sleepy sunrise in the Juarez ghetto illuminated the cloistered, ugly parts, curtained off from respectable neighborhoods.

He'd shed his clerical collar for oxford shirts, jeans, sneakers, and a starter jacket. A wardrobe he'd used as Reverend Hank. Darlene said he still looked too "preppy" and needed to dress down a bit more if he hoped to blend in.

He reveled in his new cause and would make any adaptation for the ministry. With the congressman's generosity, all was now in place. The former counselor turned clergyman turned street preacher became the Executive Director of Redemption's Corner, officially listed as a not-for-profit, non-denominational, faith-based intercessory charity, dedicated to Joanna's memory.

From her, he'd learned how the intricate web of human trafficking propelled young girls and boys to feed humankind's depravity. Whatever brought them to the street, once caught in its evil mechanizations, extrication became nearly impossible. The well-fed, small-town boy finally understood. To free one's self from muck took time, money, and contacts. Those brave enough to try too often became the bloodied victims of Juarez's revenge.

The prostitution rings snared more than a few discontented teenagers. Some ran from unhappy homes. Some were stolen from the arms of loving parents and enslaved. Because of hardened consumers, the trade flourished at the expense of ignorance and indifference. The only permanent cure rested in changed hearts. The business of prostitution, he learned, followed the rules of economy—supply and demand. Cut the demand, and the business fizzled like an extinguished candle. However, his mission was one of extrication of the providers, not exhortation of the consumer.

Many of his colleagues thought him foolish to set up a rescue mission in the heart of the jungle. But where else could he reach those most entrapped? The faces of the dead, the ones who didn't find a way out, called to him, "Please don't give up the fight."

He'd been up for over twenty hours. He headed back to the apartment. Though Aubrey's work was at night, Fischer's was during the day. They did meet for breakfast during those twilight hours when one finished his labors and the other readied to begin. Aubrey looked forward to their senseless banter, a time to compare sport stats, predict Paul's chances of joining the PGA, or rib Fischer on his inability to make a decent cup of coffee.

Aubrey sensed the tension before he opened the door to darkness. Instead of bad coffee, the air reeked of rancid cheese mingled with aged tomato sauce. He flung his coat on the couch and switched on the living room light.

What had happened here? Scraps of broken fixtures and furniture littered the carpet. He held his breath, pushed open the kitchen door and flicked on the light. Fischer sat on a stool as if in a trance, his eyes fixed on a closed pizza box.

Since childhood, the Fischer Aubrey knew suffered from mood swings not unlike those with bipolar disorder. Not severe enough to require medication, yet one never knew when Dr. Jekyll would allow Mr. Hyde to surface. Tempered by faith, his moods, appropriately channeled, tended toward the benign. After Marla's death, he chained his emotions, remained detached, until he came to DC. Over the last week, Fischer's mood had darkened. Aubrey regretted not paying more attention to the symptoms. He should have known Mr. Hyde was about to surface. What could have triggered this event?

Aubrey made a fresh pot of coffee, the gourmet blend Cynthia brought over as a housewarming gift. He placed a cup in front of Fischer. "Drink this, old man. You look like death. What happened?"

Fischer glanced upward, his eyes swollen. "I've lost her, Beaumont. I said something stupid, and now I've lost her."

Cynthia was not the kind of woman to be easily chased away by stupidity. Both he and Fischer could fill a book with the stupid things they had said. From what Aubrey had observed, Cynthia understood Fischer's lack of sophistication as part of his quirky appeal. Something else drove her away.

Aubrey put his cup on the counter. "Talk to me."

Fischer sneered and took a swig of coffee. "You're not going to like what I'm about to tell you."

What they say about the calm after the storm must be true. However, Gregg sensed his current calm was more a result of exhaustion than resolve. No telling what might happen once he confessed to Beaumont. "Better come into the living room," he said. "On second thought, maybe we should stay in the kitchen. My temper got the best of me. It's a mess in there."

"I've already seen the results of your rampage."

"I'll pay for the damages."

"We'll talk about that later."

Beaumont led the way into the other room, and Gregg stooped to pick up a broken lamp. "I'm so sorry." No apology could fix the wounds to come. He faced Beaumont who'd righted a chair and sat. "Ever have an angry outburst—the kind where you see yourself out of control but unable to stop the beast within?"

"No. Can't say that I have."

"I suppose you haven't. That I have a short fuse is no secret. I can't explain this amount of fury."

"Just let it out, friend."

After this confession, Beaumont would no longer call Gregg Fischer his friend.

Gregg paced as he talked. "I haven't been the kind of friend I should have been. I can't go back and undo the thing I most regret."

"And what's that?"

"I betrayed you."

Beaumont straightened and pierced Gregg with a hurtful glance.

The confessions poured out … how he had been paid by Congressman Curtis to provide information on Beaumont and the kids. "I should have refused. It was hard to ignore that kind of money." He sat and rubbed his face. The guilt remained. "That's not the worst of my deceit. I did find Joanna a few years back. She begged me not to tell you or anyone. She explained her parents could be in danger if they tried to contact her. She insisted you and the children were better off if you believed she was dead."

"You should have told me anyway."

"I convinced myself I only had your best interests in mind. I suppose the real reason for continued silence was the gravy train. The night I came to DC, God got a hold of me. I knew I had to tell you the truth."

"Why didn't you?"

"Joanna died, and Congressman Curtis insisted he no longer required my services after you called on him."

Why couldn't Beaumont throw a fit? There were still a few pieces of furniture he could push over or smash. His reaction was far more intimidating. He balled his fists, turned, and walked out the door.

Aubrey yawned. Exhaustion could explain some of his weariness. Not the numbness. Darlene handed him sheets and blankets for the couch. "Thanks for letting me stay here on short notice. Paul's bunking with Bradley until the wedding. There's no room for one more with all of Paul's golf equipment."

Darlene tossed him a pillow. "What happened?"

How could he explain the end of a life-long friendship when sleep begged an audience? He could scarcely comprehend its demise himself. He fluffed the pillow and wrapped up in a cocoon of blankets. "I'll explain later. I need a few hours of sleep. I have a speaking engagement at a Rotarian luncheon in a few hours. If I don't get some shut-eye, I won't make a bit of sense."

Darlene shrugged. "I have to pop over to my law office to prepare for court. I drew the drapes to keep the sun out. You look beat."

"I'll be fine. How about dinner later?"

"No need to go out. I'll bring home Chinese." She walked toward the tree. "I'll turn the lights off so you can rest better."

"No. Leave them on. I find Christmas lights calming."

She closed the door with her signature thud, so much like her mother's.

A short sofa made a very poor bed for a former basketball player. Aubrey humped his upper body on one end and let his feet dangle off the opposite arm. "It's no use." He sat up, giving his thoughts permission to flit from the furious to the burrowing—the person he most trusted took advantage of his vulnerability to cash in on his suffering. No wonder Cynthia broke up with him. Stupidity is easily forgiven—duplicity breeds distrust. She deserved better than a lying twerp. Aubrey fought against the barrage of hateful thoughts. Fatigue weakened him, and disdain danced in the muck of his despair.

He tried to pray—his words fell to the floor like bullet casings. He closed his eyes and drifted on a sea of doubt.

CHAPTER 24

Gregg drained his coffee, tossed the dirty mug into the sink, and cursed when the cup shattered. He scooped out the shards and dumped the mess into the garbage. He'd thought his rages died with the last explosion, yet the peace he craved continued to play hide and seek. How could he call himself a Christian with so much inner turmoil? Where was the promised peace that passes understanding? Maybe those miracles only happened to a chosen few, a club that apparently excluded Gregg Fischer.

Six days already. He needed to be out of this place, so Beaumont could move back in. He scurried out the apartment door with The Post tucked under his arm and opted for the stairwell … cheap exercise. Might not have a chance for a walk later. He anticipated a crammed day if Jacobs's call was any indicator, more mysterious than informative. "Got a lead," he'd said.

His Sabbath had already passed. Maybe he forgot some people worshipped on Sundays. Not that Gregg planned on church today, since he didn't know where to worship. He'd find a church as soon as he was relocated.

Though still not free of guilt, he didn't want to give up on God again as he had after Marla died. From his early days as a Christian, he'd learned that faith didn't always follow a smooth road. There were lots of challenges along the way. After Beaumont left their apartment, Gregg had spent time on his knees. He'd made a mess of things, for sure. He could only hope God would help straighten things out. Soon. At least, stop the rages and cursing. Please God, calm my spirit.

Gregg pulled out his iPhone and programed the address for the townhouse in Alexandria. Hopefully, he could move in tomorrow. He'd made the online deposit this morning. The new place would require a longer commute. At least he'd live away from a high crime area. Beaumont could have his jungle pad back. As for Gregg, he had never wanted to be that close to the natives.

He yanked open the alley door that led to his parking place and halted when he saw his rental SUV with fresh graffiti splashed across its broadside. This time the message blared: GET OUT WHILE YOU STILL CAN. Stupid artist probably didn't know the car was a rental and that Beaumont wasn't even there.

He'd wait until he moved out of this neighborhood before he bought a new vehicle. Perhaps it was a blessing he'd finally sold his car last week. If the Lexus had been parked in the alleyway, the thugs would have stolen the vehicle and left him with nothing to drive. At least this way, the mural-decorated rental would give folks something to point at. The subway exit was only a block from Briggs. But why take the Metro when he had a private parking spot in a sheltered garage?

His thoughts meandered while he darted in and out of slow moving traffic. Mostly, he mourned his rift with Beaumont. Odd how, until this blowup, two completely different personalities had managed to keep a friendship afloat for so many years. In high school, Beaumont was Mr. Popularity and had won the respect of every player on the football team as well as their opponents. Like a gentle hound, you could pull his ears, and he never growled. Whereas, Gregg's reputation tended toward impatience— fists first, talk later.

They'd always patched their differences before. This time was different.

Cynthia would know what do. If only he could call her, tell her about his fight with Beaumont. No use. Gregg sighed. He'd probably never see her or Beaumont again. In one night, he'd lost the love of his life and a life-long friend. Maybe the breakup with Cynthia would be a good thing for Beaumont. Why shouldn't he date her? No. Beaumont wouldn't. Not because of any loyalty to Gregg. He'd lost Cynthia because he refused to believe she could love a man like him, a man only one level above those Aubrey Beaumont had risked his life to save.

If he dug deeper into what motivated Gregg Fischer, he'd discover things about himself he'd rather not face. Could be money had not been the sole motivation for his deceit. Somewhere, buried in the mud of Gregg's greed, he hoped he would find Joanna, though he detested her from the moment he and Beaumont first saw her at the Top Notch.

They'd stopped by to pick up a gift package for Beaumont's parents. There she was, dressed in virginal lace, peering out the window at a fresh blanket of snow. The ethereal image didn't fool him for one moment. Beaumont, however, was taken in from the first glance. A woman alone at a romantic resort only meant trouble. Gregg had pegged her right away as a certain type—the kind who'd zoom in on a man's vulnerability. She'd sensed Beaumont's honor like a gold-digger smells wealth. Beaumont fell into her trap within minutes. Gregg had tried to warn his friend, but his suspicious rants fell on deaf ears.

Gregg continued up Constitution Avenue. As he made his way to the Brigg's building, he digested the irony. The agency initially began in Boston, prior to the Revolutionary War, with seed money from the British to spy on colonial rebels. The company opened a Washington branch after Lincoln's first inauguration. A suitable roost for the traitor he'd become.

Gregg entered his office to find Jacobs thumbing through the pile of photographs. "Morning, Jacobs. Find anything useful? You're panting over those pictures like a quarterback after a touchdown."

Jacobs handed Gregg a photo, then scattered the rest across the desk. "Take a gander. Guess I didn't imagine it after all."

"Imagine what?" Gregg settled into his chair and stared at the photograph. Not one thing jumped out as strange.

Jacobs grabbed the photo from Gregg's hand then jabbed at a red-brick building.

"A hospital ... so, what?"

"Yeah. The hospital where Dickey Jones works."

Still no sirens. "Not so strange. Pharmacists work at hospitals."

Jacobs spun around in his chair like a hyperactive five-year-old. "I finally got around to reading the Post article on your pal, Beaumont. Something you said jump-started my brain. This morning, I figured out what bugged me. So, I came down here to see if I guessed right." Jacobs manhandled the photograph like an old prospector sifts for gold. "Look more closely at the name."

Gregg could finally make out the word, "Mercy. That's significant because?"

"The hospital where Beaumont served as chaplain."

Gregg smiled. The hospital name had not registered because he never knew exactly where Beaumont worked, only that he served as a chaplain somewhere. His smirk came, however slow to comprehend, because his current case was connected to Beaumont in some way. No wonder he loved detective work. More twists in a day than a thriller novel.

"I knew your frozen Vermont brain would kick in eventually."

"Jacobs, if your hunch is right, we've found ourselves an informant."

"At the hospital?"

"Beaumont complained all the time about a blabbermouth head nurse he worked with."

Jacobs nodded. "I think I might know who you mean. I've never met her. Some of the guys have found her patient knowledge quite helpful. Rita Harrington?"

Aubrey turned over the last chair onto a rickety table and surveyed the barroom. A few moments earlier, the place had teemed with prostitutes and pimps clapping in rhythm as the praise team led a few choruses.

On Sundays, from noon to five o'clock, Mickey's Tavern turned into the Corner Chapel and welcomed those who'd come to praise God during any of three services. Aubrey suspected most of his new congregation suffered from various forms of Attention Deficit Disorder, an effect of long-term drug abuse. Others suffered from untreated bipolar or other personality disorders. Most dropped out of school at their earliest convenience or ran away from home in their early teens.

He had decided to dispense with a bulletin. Why bother when most of those attending could barely read? He discovered his worshipers responded better to shorter sermons too.

He swept under tables and around counters, not surprised at the accumulated litter left from last night's partiers. As part of the rental agreement, Aubrey promised Mickey he'd leave the bar looking better than he'd found it. With the free cleanup services, Mickey reduced the rent to almost affordable.

Aubrey pushed the crumbled napkins into a dustpan and took the debris to the alleyway where Mickey stored his dumpster. While he worked, he hummed his favorite hymn, "How Great Thou Art." Nothing like praise to make him forget every muscle in his body ached from weeks of manual labor.

Then he meandered out front to switch his church sign with Mickey's specials. When he glanced across the street, he noticed a multi-ethnic group had gathered across the street like a mixed flock of birds. They surrounded their leader, suited as expensively as a high-ranking government official, a dark-complexioned man of probable Hispanic heritage. Aubrey had never met him before, yet his regal walk, as if the asphalt owed him its right to exist, identified the man as tenement royalty. Was Joey Juarez about to make a personal visit to the newest resident of his Eastern Avenue monopoly?

Confrontation had been only a matter of time, perhaps something Aubrey even craved. As Juarez's entourage neared, Aubrey picked up a few of their Spanish words—*hombre, necessitas, muerte.*

Sometimes, he wished he carried a gun. He subdued the urge to scream, "You killed my wife. Get away from my church." How he'd love to taste the sweetness of revenge. For an instant, the fantasy tantalized. Certainly, any court would rule his murderous rage as justifiable homicide.

We all have sinned and come short of the glory of God.

Then again, sometimes the Holy Spirit pushed him against the wall with as much force as a hockey player's check. Of course, he could not kill Juarez and call himself a Christian. To do so would make him as guilty as the one he wanted to punish. "Vengeance is God's business," he whispered as Juarez crossed the street and headed toward Mickey's Bar. The Lord would avenge Joanna's murder in his own time and in his own way. If Aubrey died before knowing God finally meted justice against Joanna's killer, so be it.

If the king of Eastern Avenue needed to make a social call, one could only assume Redemption's Corner had begun to make an impact. How did Juarez plan to rid himself of this new thorn? Probably not by contract, like Joanna. Nor would Aubrey's death be by execution, a bullet in the back of the head. Juarez would not consider an enemy worthy of a quick death. Aubrey sighed, yet steeled himself for the probability … he'd be tortured.

That Juarez possessed power, none could deny. Like a satanic angel of light, this son of a Castilian model and a Columbian mobster obtained near idol status for the good his tainted wealth accomplished. Children flocked to his neighborhood center, complete with a state of the art gymnasium and skateboard park. To maintain the air of respectability and refinement, Juarez contributed large amounts to scholarship funds for those involved in his sports programs. Easy for the residents to overlook a few revenge killings when generosity flowed like a fountain.

For the moment, the mission had been allowed to exist at Juarez's pleasure, amused by its inefficiency. The reason for his non-direct opposition remained a mystery, steeped in speculation. Perhaps Juarez viewed his opponent as an annoying ant. He'd watch his victim struggle until amusement waned, then dismember the helpless creature, one appendage at a time.

Juarez said nothing as he approached. Instead, he glared his declaration of war. The spoils? The souls of the Northeast Corridor.

Aubrey squared his shoulders and prepared for battle. "Mr. Juarez, I presume?"

He smiled. His was a handsome face, no doubt the lure for many women. He presented his ultimatum in no uncertain terms. "I want you out of my area by tomorrow."

Aubrey stared back. "I'm not going anywhere."

Juarez sneered, his grayish eyes hot with purpose. He turned to his men. "I think Reverend Beaumont might need a bit more persuasion." He exhaled his words like a swine snorts—the aura of the man more to be ridiculed than feared. "You're coming with me."

At his signal, ten semi-automatic rifles pointed at Aubrey's chest.

He raised his hands. "I take it refusal would not be wise."

Brazened by his backup, Juarez poked his captive in the chest, his breath hot against Aubrey's face. "Are you a comedian too?"

"One can't resist the obvious joke." Foolish retort. One of the men smacked him across the temple with the blunt end of his Uzi, the last thing Aubrey remembered as the pavement rushed to meet his face.

CHAPTER 25

Joanna pushed away from the card table. How much solitaire could she play before her mind went completely bonkers? Lucas would not allow computer access, and he made certain the televisions were removed from the room before arrival. She paced like a lioness in wait for an open cage. How she craved to walk outside, if only for five minutes.

Casey shook his head in distain. "You must have walked off five pounds just around this room. Gimbya should be back soon with the items you asked her to buy. Maybe she'll play a game of pitch with you. Not much of a card player myself."

Joanna sat on Gimbya's bed, the one closest to the door. "Casey, have you ever experienced a premonition?"

Casey eased his chair back down. "Are you having one of them premonitions, Miss Joanna?"

Was she? Or were the imaginations mere anxiety? "For the last couple of hours, I've had strong sensations I can't explain."

"Could be the pills. Dickey said some folks might have delusions when they take them."

How could she explain something she didn't understand herself? "I've had both delusions and hallucinations when I took drugs. These feelings are very different."

"You can tell Old Casey, Miss Joanna."

"Aubrey's in trouble. I'm as sure of his peril as I am you're in this room." She fought the tears and knew what she must do. Could she find the courage?

"Maybe you're reacting to the boredom. You've been cooped up for quite a while. Besides, Juarez knows better than to whack someone like Reverend Beaumont. Your husband has powerful friends—friends who might decide to take down the whole gang."

Joanna released the torrent of tears she'd dammed up since she chose to go into witness protection. How she despised sentimentality.

"Come now, Miss Joanna. Everything will be okay."

She forced the words through her sobs. "Oh, Casey. I've been an idiot. I never should have agreed to this insane charade. I had hoped this nonsense would keep Aubrey and the children safe. Why did he have to put his charity right under Joey's nose?"

Casey handed her the box of tissues. "I'm sure you're worried over nothing."

"You don't know Joey Juarez like I do." Shame made her head droop. "When Aubrey worked the streets as Reverend Hank, Joey found Aubrey's efforts almost comedic. Joey's men gambled on how long he'd last. Aubrey fooled them all. He was one persistent missionary. He wouldn't have quit if Rita Harrington had kept her mouth shut. Redemption's Corner is different … a faith-based social program. He's drawn a line on the cement that Joey cannot ignore."

Casey shrugged his shoulders. "You have a point there, Miss Joanna."

She went to the window and looked for Gimbya's car. How much longer before she came? Joanna shivered with the cold draft that seeped through the thin walls of the motel room. If she decided to leave, she needed the coat and purse she'd asked Gimbya to buy.

She turned to face Casey. "Joey thought I was a former hooker he hired to run his prostitution ring. He never knew I had children, nor did he know my connection to Congressman Curtis. I went by the name of Joanna Carter. I worry for all those I love since he knows the truth about Aubrey. I have prayed Joey will leave them alone since he thinks I'm dead. Things seem to have only gotten worse."

Casey clicked his tongue. "I'm not supposed to talk religion while I'm at work."

"Hasn't stopped you yet, Casey. You know we're both Christians."

"I believe God's done something special for you, Miss Joanna. I also believe God will work all this out for good. That's why faith can be so hard. Sometimes we can't see what God is doing. From our view, everything seems messed up and impossible. If I've learned nothing else in my forty-year walk with the Lord, I know beyond any doubt, when things look the worst, God is doing his best."

"Do you think God will let me see my children before I die? Lucas is adamant I can't see anyone except him, you, Roberts, and Gimbya."

"Mr. Skylar's a smart man, and he'll do everything he can to protect you."

"I'm not worried about me. I'm going to die anyway. Probably very soon. The way things are, sooner might be preferable to later. Lucas knows as well as I do that I won't live long enough to testify in court. Even with the drug treatment. Why keep up the ruse?"

Casey poured two cups of coffee and handed her one. Her nerves didn't need any more caffeine, but she took his offering anyway.

"Mr. Skylar expects to take down your affidavit in a few days. These things take time to arrange. Once he has court approval and can submit your recorded testimony, if the Lord calls you home before the trial, the prosecution will have verifiable, postmortem evidence to present. If Juarez finds out you're alive, then your family would certainly be at risk. You need to stay put, Miss Joanna. Besides, your worry is unfounded. Reverend Beaumont is nothing more than a nuisance to Juarez. Not worth killing a minister. That ranks right up there with killing a cop. Juarez doesn't want the heat this close to trail."

"Trial or no trial, Joey doesn't care about cop heat. He sees himself a Caesar, deified and invincible, with an ordained right to determine who lives and dies. The new ministry challenges his omnipotence. I have to find Joey and convince him to leave Aubrey alone."

Casey glanced out the window, opened the door, and called to Roberts. "Don't forget to check the perimeter." He sat back down in his chair and rocked. "Look, Mr. Skylar will be awful mad if you run out, Miss Joanna. Besides, you're in no condition to go very far. Trust the Lord to watch over Reverend Beaumont."

Professionally said with a Christian current. Casey's duty required dissuasion. Though he chose to deny his instinct, deep down he must know what she knew. Her only trump card was surrender. She'd find Joey, bargain for Aubrey's life. Though evil incarnate, Joey possessed one solitary virtue. Once his word was given, he would never go back on his promise.

Perhaps she'd find purpose in her death—an answer to the prayer she uttered the day she found the Lord. If Aubrey lived, her prayer would be answered.

"Help me, please, Casey. Witness Protection is supposedly a volunteer program."

Casey shook his head. "True, Miss Joanna. I won't lie to you. Thing is, your protection, and your family's protection, depends upon your cooperation with the terms of the agreement. You leave, and everything's off the table. Stay here, Miss Joanna. Where would you go? Who would take care of you?"

"I'm not without resources, and I'm not without friends."

Casey stood, his rigid stance like an accusatory finger. "Bad friends. Bad money. You should at least wait for Mr. Skylar. Maybe he can find another hospice center for you. Someplace where you can come and go as you want and where someone will look after your needs. I'm sure he'd do that for you."

Joanna kept discreet silence.

"You've a mind to go back to Juarez, don't you?"

She couldn't wait for Gimbya any longer. "I'm going, Casey. Legally, you can't stop me."

"No, I can't. I'll do what I can to smooth things over with Mr. Skylar, in case you change your mind. May I give you a hug goodbye?"

She kissed his chubby cheek then walked out the door.

Lucas Skylar took another sip of beer as he yelled at the quarterback from the comfort of his living room couch. How he enjoyed Sunday afternoon football. What was Joanna doing to fill the hours? Hopefully, nothing too strenuous. She'd showed some improvement with the drug, but over the last couple days she seemed to spiral backward. Judge Woolsey was supposedly willing to record her testimony in a few days … as a precaution, since she might not survive until the trial. Likely, though, her words would be thrown out by any competent defense attorney, and Juarez would have an army of them at his disposal.

His emergency cell chimed. Now what. He checked the ID. Casey.

"Mr. Skylar, Miss Joanna left."

"What do you mean, she left?"

"I tried to talk her out of it, sir."

"Out of what?'

"She wanted to leave witness protection. Says she's worried about her husband. Said she had a premonition."

"You weigh three times more than her, and you couldn't stop her?"

Casey groaned. "It's her right, Mr. Skylar. The program's voluntary."

"Yeah, yeah. I suppose there was nothing you could do on that score. Look, I'll get an arrest warrant. Part of her plea deal was her testimony at trial."

"I slipped a tracker in her sweater pocket. But I've lost the signal. She must have discovered the device and thrown it away."

"Go after her. She couldn't have gone very far. I'll call you as soon as it's legal to slap handcuffs on her."

CHAPTER 26

Gregg smiled as Jacobs charmed Rita Harrington with all the grace of a cobra tamer. "I see you are quite dedicated to your work," he cooed. "We won't take up much of your valuable time." He showed Rita the same picture he'd shoved in Gregg's face earlier. "You seem as observant as you are beautiful, Nurse Harrington. May I call you Rita?"

She blinked her eyes like a flirtatious geisha waves a fan.

"Have you ever seen this person?" Jacobs propped his elbow on the counter.

She unleashed her stethoscope from her neck while she leaned in to examine the picture. Her arm rested next to Jacobs's elbow. Before Gregg could bat an eye, Jacobs stroked Rita's hand. "I don't see a ring."

Rita blushed. "I'm not married."

"Oh, but there must be a special someone in your life … a woman as beautiful as you."

"No … no one special."

"That's good news for me, then. I notice we both like cinnamon tea. Maybe we could meet at the deli for a cup and see what other things we have in common."

She gave her number to Jacobs, and he tucked the yellow post-it into his shirt pocket. "I'll call." He winked. "Soon."

How does one keep a straight face with Romeo at his best? Whatever magic Jacobs tossed, Rita gushed with enough information about Dickey Jones to write a full-length biography.

She pulled her shoulders back, her cheeks hot with pride. "It's been a boost for the hospital to have one of our own involved with King Pharmaceutical's latest test project, though the drug is only used for end-stage treatment."

"End stage?" Jacobs played clueless to perfection.

"When there is no other treatment and death is expected within three to six months. The medication holds great promise for hospice patients."

Jacobs leaned on the counter. "How does the drug help?"

"No curative impact, of course. However, patients report a better quality of life. They are stronger which allows the patient to take walks or go for car rides. Nothing too strenuous but able to be out of bed for longer periods of time. The drug dulls the pain without drowsiness or reduced respiration. In some cases, the medication is known to extend life. Dr. Jones says the preliminary trials have been quite promising. Of course, he has complete control over the program. I know he hopes for FDA approval soon. In fact, a few weeks ago, I saw him in conversation with Lucas Skylar from the US Attorney's office."

Gregg veered a glance toward Jacobs. What business did Lucas Skylar have in a drug scheme?

Jacobs leaned in as close as Rita would allow. The extra attention worked, or had Jacobs moved from prodding a witness to a genuine interest in Dragon Lady? Why not? Stranger matches happened every day. "There's someone for everyone," so the adage says. Why not Jacobs and "The Gossip of Mercy Hospital?"

Gregg lured Jacobs away with an urgent plea, one he hoped Rita might understand. "Don't forget the game this afternoon, Jacobs. I got fifty on the home team."

Jacobs eased away but kept his gaze toward Rita. "Busy tomorrow?"

She smiled. One would think a face as tight as hers would crack with a grin that broad. "I'm off."

Gregg pointed toward the elevator. He and Jacobs reviewed what they had learned thus far. "It is no accident Lucas Skyler's name popped up. Every instinct I have tells me he's connected to Jones … and not on the up and up."

Cynthia closed the suitcase and tucked the stray strand of hair behind her ear.

"Done packin' my things?"

She jumped. "I didn't know you were in the room, Dad."

She put the suitcase on the floor with his two boxes of possessions and memories.

His nursing home placement could not have come at a better time. She needed to leave Silver Spring as soon as possible. Maybe once she returned to Chicago, she could put Gregg Fischer out of her mind. How foolish she'd been to think she might have a future with him.

The placement would be beneficial for Dad, his care needs far beyond what she could provide. How sad she found her father only to lose him to a cruel disease. How much of her would he remember in a month or two?

She drew comfort from the fact she'd remember him long after he forgot her.

"Now, where am I going again, little girl?"

"Farrington House, Dad. I'm sure you'll like the place. There's a special room for sports fanatics like you. You can watch ESPN all day."

"Expect everyone will know where to find me. I sure hope I see Pastor Aubrey, even though he ain't my pastor anymore. I like that Gregg feller too."

Did Dad have to mention Gregg? "Aubrey promised he'd look in on you for me."

Dad sat on his bed. "Don't look so sad. I'm not afeared, Cindy."

"I know you'll do fine at Farrington House. I'm sad because I have to leave you so soon."

"Don't have to. House is yours."

"Yes, I know. We added my name to the deed. At one point, I thought I might stay here permanently. Help Aubrey with his new ministry. I think I need to go back to Chicago."

"You'll sell the house then?"

"Probably. If you want me to."

"You do what you think is best. You'll come see me again?"

"I'll come for a visit in the summer when school is out. I put in for early retirement."

"Then why go back to Chicago?"

"I have friends. A good church. I'll substitute."

"Got all that here in Silver Spring."

I don't have Gregg. Her former life would help her forget him … no reminders as there would be here … the restaurants where they ate or the golf courses they trekked … and the cold walk on the beach at Chesapeake Bay. Though only here a few weeks, she'd stored enough memories for a lifetime.

"I'll visit as often as I can, Dad." Soon, you won't miss me, though I'll miss you terribly. "We're all the family either one of us has. I won't let go of the memories we've made. I promise."

"I know you won't, Cindy. Too bad you and Gregg are on the outs. I liked him."

"Wasn't meant to be, Dad."

"What happened?"

How could she answer him? Dad held both Aubrey and Gregg in high regard. Let him hold on to those good thoughts.

Her phone vibrated, and she checked the caller ID. Darlene. Good. A reprieve from Dad's persistent questioning. "This is Cynthia."

"Glad I got you. I'm worried about Aubrey. We were supposed to meet at Mickey's to go over mission paperwork for tomorrow's board meeting. He's not here. Not like him to be late for any meeting. You could set your clock by him. Do you know where he might have gone?"

"No. Did you try Gregg?"

"He doesn't answer his cell. Aubrey's been staying with me until Gregg moves out of the apartment. Probably in the next day or two."

"Why would Gregg move out?"

"Aubrey said they had some sort of argument, but that's all he'd say."

"Friends have arguments all the time. Maybe Aubrey went to see Gregg to work things out. Wouldn't be surprised if they decided to discuss their differences over a round of golf."

"Neither one of them has returned my messages."

Cynthia breathed out to remain calm. Darlene needn't sense more anxiety.

"Maybe Aubrey went to Redemption's Corner and lost track of time? Gregg is probably at work and can't return calls for some reason."

"I called the landline at the mission. No answer. Besides, Aubrey doesn't lose track of time. I'm really worried, Cynthia"

You're not the only one. "Maybe there's something wrong with the phone."

"The phone worked earlier today."

"Look. I'm taking my father to the nursing home. Be about an hour. If you still haven't heard from Aubrey by then, I'll meet you at the mission. Hang tight and trust God for Aubrey's safety."

"What if something has happened to him, Cynthia? I don't think I can stand to lose him. He's the only father I've ever known."

CHAPTER 27

Aubrey squinted as he came to. Bile burnt his throat and demanded escape. Where was he? He fought the chains wrapped around him like yards of cord. A voice from somewhere echoed through the room. A man talked into a cell. "Mr. Juarez, Reverend Beaumont is awake."

Aubrey pulled on his chains. No use. Tethered like an animal to something like a post.

"You're wasting your time, Reverend Beaumont." A young Hispanic man approached as he pocketed his cell. He jabbed the tip of a Bushmaster .223 into Aubrey's rib cage. The weapon surprised Aubrey, since he heard many gangs were reverting to handguns. Easier to manage and conceal.

Ludicrous. Instead of fear, Aubrey marveled at the extent of Juarez's armament and wondered that a man of peace like himself recognized the weapon. The lone cop on his board insisted Aubrey take a crash course on gang weaponry in addition to street drug identification. A month ago, he wouldn't have known an assault rifle from a machine gun or meth from heroin.

The door creaked opened, and Juarez joined the young Hispanic man. "My apologies for your rough treatment, Reverend Beaumont."

Aubrey groaned.

"Leave us, Ramón."

Ramón hesitated, like a child unwilling to leave a parent. "Mr. Juarez, you are unarmed."

Aubrey grinned. "As you can see, Ramón, I pose no threat to your boss."

Juarez laughed. At Aubrey or Ramón? "Reverend Beaumont has only his words to use against me. Go."

The young man clipped hesitant steps as he exited, leaving Aubrey alone to face his nemesis.

"I don't think you brought me here for casual conversation."

"I knew you were a smart man, Reverend Beaumont."

"My parishioners call me Pastor Aubrey. You may call me Aubrey. My closest friends address me simply as Beaumont."

"I prefer the formality of your position. I respect the clergy."

"Is that why you've chained me up like an animal? Not how I'd define respect."

"I apologize; however, my men insisted I take precautions."

"What are you afraid of?"

Juarez sprang from his chair and punched Aubrey in the stomach. "I'm not afraid of anything, least of all you. Are we clear?"

Aubrey offered a weak nod.

"Like I said. I have no wish to harm a man of the cloth. However, you have put me in a very difficult position."

"How's that."

"Seems some of my people are convinced you can give them something I cannot."

"Not me. The Lord."

"I don't believe in this Lord of yours. However, your words have confused my workers. You see, I'm a businessman. If you were a rival drug dealer, I would not have bothered to try to negotiate."

"I suppose not."

Juarez tugged on his suit coat. Nervousness? "I brought you here to offer you a deal. Cooperate and you'll live."

"You said it yourself. I only have words to use against you."

Juarez's laugh pierced Aubrey's eardrums. "We've had more than a few do-gooders on Eastern Avenue. We found them to be a source of entertainment. They like to parade around with Bibles and food. They might manage to convince a few of my workers to try to leave our organization. We caught some of those deserters and used them to teach the others a lesson. Some escaped. I counted them as acceptable losses."

"Why do you fear me … wrong word … why do find my work less amusing now?"

Juarez tilted forward. "You're organized."

Aubrey risked a snort. "We're a threat? Good. I prayed we would be."

"You have support from important people. If important people become interested, the cops become interested. Wouldn't be long before I'm out of business. A scenario I don't much like. Don't you see my predicament? I need to put a stop to your little mission."

"You don't scare me, Juarez."

"Brave words, Reverend Beaumont." Juarez squatted and whispered into Aubrey's ear. "You have children, don't you? A daughter, Darlene is an attorney. You also have a son, Paul, who plays golf, and another son, Bradley. Congratulations on his engagement. You will soon have a daughter-in-law to add to your family. Lovely girl, Trish, don't you think? How am I doing?"

Aubrey pulled against the chains, his volcanized rage insufficient to free him. "Why, you—"

"I really have no wish to harm you or your children or your friends. However, if you persist … you leave me with few options. I'll give you a few minutes to consider what I've said. I suggest you listen to my offer of peace and leave my territory. If you must play with your charity, you have my permission to locate your mission elsewhere. Ruin someone else's enterprises."

"Or?"

"Trust me, the alternatives are very unpleasant."

The sun started its descent. Gregg poked Jacobs in the ribs, in case he'd fallen asleep. "There he is."

They'd waited for hours in front of Skylar's house, passing the binoculars back and forth like a couple of hunters in a duck blind. Their fowl friend finally on the move, Gregg waited for Skylar to get into his vehicle.

Of all the times to rush off without a GPS tracker, like a couple of amateurs.

Skylar zigzagged through residential areas. Either he knew someone followed him or he had practiced diversion as a just-in-case scenario.

"I think Skylar made us. Glad you're at the wheel, Jacobs. I'm not that familiar with DC yet."

Jacobs laughed. "Skylar only thinks he's cagey. I've followed trickier dudes than him. He drives like a man with a lot on his mind. Distracted drivers are the easiest to follow."

Skylar turned onto Eastern Avenue, then stopped and got out of his car. As they neared, he waved at them.

Gregg's turn to laugh. "Told ya."

Jacobs cell chimed.

"Skylar?"

"I knew you were behind me, Jacobs. Let's talk."

As Jacobs opened his door, he leaned toward Gregg. "He thinks we're a couple of idiots. Can't believe he called me on his cell. I just cloned it. Like I said. He's distracted."

Gregg and Jacobs got out of their car and approached Skylar. "Is this your new partner, Jacobs?"

Gregg shook Skylar's hand. "Gregg Fischer."

"Mr. Fischer." Unspoken recognition flowed through his grip and welled in his too careful gaze.

"What do I owe the pleasure of your attention, gentlemen?"

Jacobs leaned against Skylar's car. "Curiosity."

"Can you be more specific?"

"We have a client that is concerned about a doctor whom we think you know."

"I know a lot of doctors."

Gregg followed Jacob's lead. "Dickey Jones?"

"Yes. I've heard of him. What trouble is he into now?"

"Our client is concerned about the way Dickey manages his clinical trial programs. Seems there has been some irregular activity. You wouldn't happen to know anything about that?"

"No."

"We think you do."

"Proof?"

"Not yet. Other than a witness who overheard you discussing the program with Dr. Jones. Now what interest would you have in this particular program?"

Skylar glared. "Look, I'm busy. I have no time for your games, Jacobs. If you have an accusation to make, make it. Otherwise, I'll be on my way. If you follow me again, I'll report you for harassment." He pocketed his cell. "Don't bother listening to my calls. I'm getting rid of this one soon as I get into the car."

Gregg squared his shoulders. "I don't think it's a coincidence that Dickey's drug helps terminally ill cancer patients. Is it possible you have a star witness you hope will live a little longer? Is that why you are pals with Dickey Jones?"

Jacobs squished his brows together. Gregg smiled. He probably should have mentioned his suspicions to his partner, that Skylar might have fabricated Joanna's death.

Skylar's face paled. "Maybe I asked Dickey about his program to get information for a friend."

Gregg peered at Skylar. "That friend wouldn't happen to be Joanna Beaumont?"

Skylar's face turned from white to scarlet. He pulled Gregg's coat by the lapels. "What makes you think I know Mrs. Beaumont apart from her connection to Juarez?"

"I happen to be her husband's best friend. I've tracked Joanna for years. I know you dated her in college, and that you are most likely Darlene's father."

Jacobs whistled. "Darlene Beaumont? Your kid, Lucas? Interesting."

Skyler pushed Jacobs against the car. "Not as interesting as your sorry face will look like if you don't forget this conversation."

Gregg smirked. Only guilty people reacted violently. His suspicions had been right. "Don't worry. Aubrey doesn't know for sure. Your secret's still safe. Just tell me where I can find Joanna."

"Your friend has her ashes. Ask him."

"Don't think they're her ashes, Skylar."

"Wonderful fiction, Fischer. You should write a book."

Gregg took two steps toward Skylar. "Consider this. If we figured out Joanna's alive, you can be sure Juarez will. Or maybe you don't care at this point. I'd bet my last dollar you've managed to obtain certified affidavits, so her testimony can be entered posthumously."

Skylar waved his Glock. "Time you gentlemen got on your way, don't you think?"

Jacobs motioned Gregg to back off. "No need for violence, Mr. Skylar. Seems like we have all the intel we need. Have a nice day, Counselor."

When they returned to Jacobs's car, he grabbed the wheel. "You really think your friend's wife is still alive?"

"I do."

"So ... now what?"

"We've got enough to report to our client. If you don't mind doing the paperwork, I have something else that needs my attention. Technically Sunday is my day off."

Jacobs chuckled. "You're going to follow Skylar again. What gives?"

"Long story. Let's just say, I need to find out if Joanna's alive or not. I owe Beaumont. If my suspicions are right, Skylar has her under wraps."

Gregg checked his cell. He'd had it on mute during the stakeout and missed two calls from Darlene and a text from Cynthia. *No one can find Aubrey. The board has met at the mission for prayer. Darlene is with me.*

He cringed with worry. Impossible no one knew Beaumont's whereabouts unless he was in trouble. An accident maybe? Beaumont carried a list of contact numbers in his wallet. If he'd been hurt or unconscious someone would have heard. Unless ...

Jacobs jabbed Gregg's shoulder. "You look gray in the gills, Fischer."

"A text from Cynthia."

"Your girl?"

"Used to be."

"What happened?"

"We broke up. I acted like the jerk I am."

"Must be you're a supersized jerk for her to call it quits. I could tell that girl was crazy about you. What did she want? To give you a second chance?"

"I wish. No. She's worried about Beaumont. No one knows where he is. That man wears responsibility like some women wear mink. He prides himself on punctuality."

"People change."

"Not Beaumont. His board has gathered for a prayer vigil."

Panic consumed him. Premonition? He'd had one in Afghanistan ... an inexplicable sense of doom. A few minutes later, his unit was caught in a hailstorm of bullets. He lost three of his men and took shrapnel to his leg. Missed the femoral artery by a quarter of an inch.

He'd warned Beaumont not to tango in Juarez territory. The crazy do-gooder looked the bull in the eye, waved a red flag, and dared the beast to charge. Every instinct told Gregg that Juarez had accepted the challenge.

Gregg replied to Cynthia's text: *Got your message. Have a hunch. Will call soon.*

Jacobs speared him with an inquisitive glance. "I'll regret this. But, where to?"

"How well do you know Juarez territory?"

"Some say I'm an expert. Why?"

"Going after Beaumont. I think he and Juarez are having a showdown."

"Are you psychic?"

"No. But I know Beaumont."

Jacobs shook his head. "This is insane. What about the preacher's wife?"

"If Skylar has her, at least she's safe. I need to find Beaumont first."

Jacobs pulled his black sedan onto the street. "Takes crazy to partner with crazy. Let's roll."

CHAPTER 28

Lucas trembled as he ran a nervous hand through his hair. He pulled out his emergency cell from the glove compartment and called Casey.

"Found her yet?"

"We've been on her tail. She just went into the subway."

"Arrest her at your first opportunity. I have the warrant. Skylar out."

He'd pushed Joanna too hard. He cared what happened to her. She did have the right to leave the program regardless of what he thought best for all concerned. However, once she left, she forfeited protection, including hospice care. Arrest, as ironic as it seemed, was the only option to help her.

His phone chimed. Casey. "She got off on Eastern Avenue, but I lost her. These tenements are like underground tunnels. She could be in any one of them."

"Keep looking. Get backup if you need to."

"Do you think she might be looking for Joey Juarez? Suicide if she is. If she thinks she can strike up a deal with her old boyfriend, she's crazy. You can't negotiate with a rattle snake."

"I hope not. Just in case, I'll see if I can finagle a warrant on Juarez too."

"Can't you let her go, Mr. Skylar? She doesn't have long. I hate to think of her dying in prison."

"Don't get soft on me, Casey. Do your job."

"Yes, Mr. Skylar."

Juarez held several properties near Beaumont's mission. Could be Joanna decided to run back to Juarez. Not surprised. The vixen used men like disposable gloves. She probably needed a fix so bad, she'd risk anything. Although, if this conversion of hers was real, perhaps she thought she could cut a deal with Juarez to spare Beaumont. Would she be that foolish? Juarez would take revenge against his own mother if he thought she'd turned on him. How much more would he do to Joanna? If she showed how much she cared about Beaumont, Juarez would pop him for spite, let alone his infringement upon Juarez territory. Nothing good would come from her sacrifice.

Lucas raised eyes toward Heaven. If God existed, maybe he'd let a sinner help a saint … find Joanna before she found Juarez. She'd be safer in prison than on the street.

He'd loved her once, as much as a selfish ambitious law student could love anyone. How did Fischer know about their history? Unless, Joanna had told him? Or, he'd found out from her parents that they'd dated. Not hard to do the math on Darlene.

So many years later, Joanna still touched his soul, and he despised the emotion she brought to the surface. He had no room for sentimentality if he were to realize his dream for a political career.

If Juarez knew Joanna was still alive, Darlene would be at risk too. Juarez would demand Joanna suffer. He'd make no agreement with a sacrificial lamb. Lucas laughed as he mused. Funny how a few months can change a man. When Joanna called him for help, he only embraced the opportunity to take down a drug lord. Now, his daughter's face loomed before him.

CHAPTER 29

Cynthia raised her head at the sound, like a crash, as if the downstairs door had been forced open. A thud followed, then unintelligible shouts mingled with hurried footsteps in the stairwell. All present exchanged nervous glances. Cynthia whispered her orders as loudly as she dared. "Turn off the lights. Everyone, go into the back room. I'll call the police." She punched in 911 as she joined the others.

They huddled in silence as the quake of obscenities from the other room reverberated off the walls. As quickly as the horde had entered, sounds of retreat eased their fears until all that could be heard were the heartbeats of nervous board members.

Cynthia opened the door and flicked on the lights. "Does anyone else smell smoke?"

Heads shook as Cynthia spotted billowing flames coming from the main room.

"We've got to get out of here. Now." *Lord, you kept Shadrach, Meshach, and Abednego safe in the fiery furnace. Do you think you could keep us safe and lead us out of this firetrap?*

Gregg stood in the alleyway at the back entrance to Juarez's building and gagged at the blood-stained pavement. He thought war had hardened him, but instead, he turned and vomited. He'd been held prisoner by Iraqi dissidents and forced to watch as they beheaded the soldier captured with him—left to wonder if he'd be next. Fortunately for him, his unit rescued him, too late to save his fellow prisoner.

Here he stood on a different battlefield.

Why couldn't a civilized society put a stop to street crime? Certainly, there were more good guys than bad guys. Perhaps war-wearied civil servants had become hardened to the atrocities committed in these inner-city cesspools birthed by indifference. Let the slums rule the slums.

Awareness dawned. Beaumont's campaign had not been against the suppliers. Rather, he fought to deliver those caught in the web of apathy. Gregg breathed a vow. If God helped him find Beaumont, he'd join his fight in spirit, not merely in deed.

Apprehension threatened his faith. A criminal mind like Juarez's would do one of two things with his captive—take him for an immediate ride and dump his body in the Potomac or extract information via torture before the ride. He dismissed the devil's option and hoped instead for the deep blue sea. At least, the later bought Beaumont time.

Jacobs glanced toward the roof. "Rumors are Juarez uses this building as his headquarters. The place is essentially abandoned otherwise. If he is holding your friend, chances are this is where we'll find him."

He and Jacobs searched for a point of entry. When they paused to look for unbarricaded doors, a rat nibbled at Gregg's shoelace. He kicked it aside, and it scrambled toward a dumpster. Gregg followed its movement and spotted a basement window, picked up a piece of broken cement, and smashed the glass.

An alarm blared, and the two ducked behind the dumpster. Jacobs scowled. "You want to get us killed? That was a rookie mistake, Fischer."

"We'll wait until the goons come out in search of the intruder, and we'll sneak in."

"And you got this idea from which movie?"

He handed Jacobs a second large piece of cement. "If there are only two goons, you hit one and I'll smack the other."

"And what if they find us first?"

"Do you have your gun handy?"

Jacobs released the safety as three men ran out of the building, assault rifles readied. He signaled toward the door. "Storm the castle, Sherlock. I'll distract them … take them on a chase."

"What if they catch you?"

"They won't. You forget. I know this area."

Gregg took out his revolver. "Be careful."

Jacobs pushed Gregg forward. "Speak for yourself. Go."

Gregg climbed four flights of stairs, hope diminishing as he spotted more goons—six or more on the first floor alone. How would he find Beaumont without alerting Juarez's army? Maybe he should find Juarez, first. Save the government the cost of a trial, then call the police. Good plan if Gregg Fischer were the kind to listen to his own advice.

Fractured light from a streetlamp seeped through an occasional window as shadows danced against mildewed walls. Perspiration beaded on his forehead. The last step led to a large open area. He flattened himself against a wall and scanned the room. There … on the other side … a man chained to what looked like a post, his head drooped. Beaumont? Gregg pursed his lips. Was he too late?

Joanna leaned against the wall adjacent to Joey's den. She straightened with determination. At first, he'd likely laugh at her ghostly reappearance. And he might have Ramón shoot her on the spot before she could plead Aubrey's cause. She put her hand on the knob. Unlocked. She listened. Too quiet. Joey probably wasn't in there. Should she wait for him outside?

She fell back into the shadows at the sound of hurried steps. Ramón led the way while Joey followed a safe six paces behind. With exaggerated bravery, she pushed herself into their path.

Ramón raised his weapon, but Joey pushed the rifle aside. "Look what the devil brought us, Ramón. A ghost."

"Say the word, Mr. Juarez. I won't miss this time."

"Not yet. First, let's see if she's real or a figment of both our imaginations."

Ramón ripped her blouse and felt along her upper torso. "She doesn't seem to be wired. I'll check elsewhere to be sure."

Joanna dared to slap his hand away. "Keep your filthy hands off me." She defied the cough curdled in her throat.

Joey laughed. "I see your cancer has not robbed you of spunk." He waved Ramón away, pulled her toward him, and twisted her arm. She expected he'd snap her neck and be done with her. Instead he released his grip and stroked her chin. The man, a complex bag, as tender as he was vicious. "Why are you here? Need a fix? Think I'll forgive you and take you back like nothing happened?"

"I don't do drugs anymore, Joey. I've changed."

He pushed her against the wall. Soon, he'd unleash the whole of his brutality. "People like you and me never change, Joanna. You betrayed your husband like you betrayed me."

She met his hateful glance. "Aubrey is the reason I'm here."

"What makes you think I care about him?"

"He's challenged you. He represents a force against which you cannot stand."

"What force?"

"God."

His hard slap knocked her to the floor. As if angel arms lifted her, she found the strength to stand. "Joey, please. Leave Aubrey alone."

"I will not cower to a religious freak. However, I think maybe the good pastor and I have reached an agreement."

"How's that?"

"I've shown myself to be the better man. I have given him an out. I don't wish to kill a man of the cloth. I will, if I must, and bear the consequence of police retaliation."

"And you don't fear the Lord?"

"You can't fear what you don't believe."

"If you harm him, the police will have no choice but to raid your territory. The outcry would be heard across the country. He's famous now, you know."

"I watch the news. That's why I tried to reason with him. If he leaves my neighborhood, I won't kill your children."

"You monster!" She flailed at him with balled fists. Joey punched her in the chest and sent her to the floor in agony. This time she was unable to rise. Would she die now? Useless? Unable to save Aubrey, her children, or anyone else?

Joey squatted and fondled her hair with feigned tenderness. He gazed up at Ramón. "What shall I do with this traitor?"

Ramón positioned his trigger finger. "I have an idea."

"No. Don't be in a hurry, my friend. She doesn't deserve a quick death."

She sneered. "You think cancer is quick? I don't care what you do to me."

He stood. "Maybe I'll tie you up along with your precious Aubrey. You can die together."

"He's here?"

"My guest for the moment."

"I know how you treat your guests."

"Maybe I'll let you watch while I cut him to pieces. Then I'll let you rot beside his remains."

No words would come, his intent too horrible to ponder.

"Tie her up, Ramón. Then we'll have another talk with Reverend Beaumont."

Once his eyes adjusted to the darkness, Gregg scanned the room. No sign of any one besides Beaumont. Gregg crawled to the closest wall, pulled himself to a standing position and inched his way further into the room, relieved when he heard Beaumont's moan.

Hastening his pace, Gregg carefully inched his way toward Beaumont, using the dark shadows on the wall as cover. He felt a door with his left hand, then groped his way past until he reached Beaumont. Satisfied they were alone, he pulled out his silencer, shot off the lock, then unraveled the chains.

Beaumont opened his eyes. "Glad to see you, old friend."

"Can you walk?"

He winced as he nodded.

"Let's go." Gregg pulled Beaumont to the landing, then brought him to a stand. "Be careful, these steps are steep."

The back door squeaked, followed by a hum from the overhead florescent light. Gregg shoved Beaumont into a nook as two shadowy figures emerged from the doorway. One held a rifle at his side. The suited man must be Juarez. Gregg whispered to Beaumont. "Stay there. We've got company, and of the two of us, I'm the only one with a gun."

"I'll only slow you down. Get out while you can."

"Fat chance."

Juarez glanced toward the fallen chains and slammed his fist against the wall. "Ramón, find him."

Gregg emerged from the alcove, his revolver poised. He couldn't take them both but hoped he'd get Juarez before Ramón got off a shot. "Not so fast, Juarez."

The two men froze. Gregg aimed at Juarez and pulled back the trigger.

Someone tackled him from behind—the gun fired into the air, missing its target. Without hesitation, Ramón readied to fire. A shrill laugh preceded Juarez's command. "Put it away, Ramón!"

Beaumont lay on the floor and gasped for air as Gregg pulled himself to a stand. "I had them. I had them both."

"Couldn't let you kill anyone because of me. And Mr. Juarez is unarmed."

Juarez stepped forward. "Reverend Beaumont, you are either very brave or very stupid. I haven't decided which." He raised his hand with the authority of a shrewd dictator. "Ramón, escort our company outside."

Gregg smiled in disbelief. "You're letting us go?"

"Mr. Fischer—"

"You know who I am?"

"In any war, one must know his enemy as well as his enemy's friends. You might think me a man with no honor. You're wrong. Even someone like me cannot kill a man who has just saved his life. You are spared, only because of your friendship with such a man as Reverend Beaumont. Yes. I'm letting you go. For now. Don't test my patience, Reverend. Next time, I won't owe you."

Ramón led them down the front stairwell to the street. Smoke fouled the air, the night heated by the blaze from the next block down. "This is as far as I go. Look there. Your mission is about to crumble. You've been warned. Leave this neighborhood or die."

Gregg's eyes misted. "Beaumont, the board members are in there."

CHAPTER 30

Time rolled into time as she lay in a heap on Joey's floor like refuse. How foolish she'd been. Her efforts to save Aubrey merely fueled Joey's determination to kill him.

An undefined presence hovered above. Angels? Peace calmed her fears though pain beyond measure seared through every nerve. The end was near. Let the Lord orchestrate these next few hours as he saw fit. Whatever the outcome, she could do nothing more than trust Sovereign God's mercy.

Joey stormed into the room, kicked over the chairs, and punched the walls while he spewed curses in three languages.

Joanna smiled. His rage, like that of a thwarted demon, meant his scripted plan had unraveled. Aubrey was alive.

After Joey spent his rage, he slumped onto the floor next to her. "Your idiotic husband saved my life. Why? His friend, the private investigator, had me in his sights, and I saw the Hell where your God would send me."

"I'm sorry Gregg missed."

"He never got the chance. Reverend Beaumont sacked him."

Joanna laughed … the irony too precious. The King of 20th Street saved by the man he most determined to hate. "Poor Joey."

In days gone by, she would have feared his retaliation at her amusement. The dying can afford to be reckless. If he beat her to death, she'd consider his blows acts of mercy. Aubrey lived. Nothing left to do now but die.

Joey stroked her hair with unexpected gentleness. "Perhaps this will better suit my purposes. I see how this disease tortures you. Worse than anything I could do to you. A few days, perhaps a week? Who knows?" He cocked his head. "You believe me a monster and rightly so. Know this. I loved you, Joanna."

"You're incapable of love, Joey."

"Perhaps."

He caressed her, raised her to her feet, kissed her, then shoved her against the wall. "Get out. Before I come to my senses."

Cynthia handed each board member a wet towel. "Cover your head and breathe as little as possible." Smoke and flames filled the office and blocked the front exit where the fire had been set. The group retreated to the back, still free from smoke, and climbed down the fire escape to the alley below.

They ran to the street and were ushered to a blocked off area while firefighters sprayed a hopeless cascade of water. Too late to save Redemption's Corner, the structure now a wall of red, white, and yellow. Cracks and hisses echoed the building's imminent collapse. At least everyone had evacuated.

The barricaded expanse could barely contain the crowds that had poured out to observe the death of the tenement. She scanned the hordes with anxious hope. Like a dream, Aubrey and Gregg approached the barricade, quickly pushed into the crowds by police. She wormed her way toward them. "Aubrey. What happened?"

She took the wet towel that had protected her face and wiped the blood from Aubrey. A gash spread about a quarter of an inch across his cheek. "You need stitches."

Gregg gave her a wounded glance. "I'll make sure he gets to the ER."

Aubrey gently removed her hand. "I'm not going anywhere. Not until I know everyone's okay."

"Gregg, how did you find him?"

He snickered. "I'm a private detective, remember? I detected."

A bearded man sidled up next to Gregg. "I see your instincts paid off." He shook Aubrey's hand. "The name's Jacobs, Gregg's partner."

Gregg hugged the man. "Beaumont, I couldn't have found you without this man's help. I was afraid I'd have to go find him next."

"Like I said, Fischer, I know the area like my own backyard. Sorry about your mission, Reverend Beaumont. I called Rabbi Gruber who leads the temple on Allison Street. He's been interested in what you're trying to do here and wants to help you rebuild."

Congressman Curtis ambled toward Aubrey and shook a fist at the ruins. "If Juarez wants war, we'll give it to him. I just talked to the police chief and the mayor. It's time to clean up this neighborhood."

Joanna leaned against a lamppost and gasped for breath. Flames shot from a building the next block over. Redemption's Corner? If Joey's men set the blaze, that would explain his sudden compassion. He had no need to kill her or Aubrey. In Joey's warped mind, no building meant no mission. He was unable to see a God whose ability to save needed no earthly address.

Sirens wailed in the background—four police cars careened to a stop next to Joey's headquarters. She could only assume more went into the alley and surrounded him.

Too tired to cry, she slid to the pavement. *Nothing I did made a difference, Lord. Why did you let me live to see the futility of my prayer? Aubrey saved himself, and Lucas only has an unsubstantiated recorded testimony to use against Joey's attorneys. Is this my last hurrah—a useless attempt at martyrdom?*

She stayed propped against the tree until Redemption's Corner collapsed. She prayed Aubrey had not escaped Joey only to die in the flames. How she wanted to find him. To be in his arms one last time.

Though a few blocks away, Redemption's Corner might as well have been a hundred miles. She slid to the pavement too weak to crawl another foot. Within her soul, a demonic voice railed songs of defeat. *It's too late, Joanna. Curl up and die. You deserve a bitter end.*

Gregg watched in disbelief as Redemption's Corner collapsed. "Beaumont, I'm so sorry."

"A ministry is far more than a building, Fischer. People are the foundation by which God's work succeeds or fails."

Lucas Skylar emerged from the row of police cars. "Reverend Beaumont, I'm glad you're okay. I saw you here and thought you should know that Juarez has been arrested on weapons charges. You don't need to worry about him for the time being. He blabbered something about you. Looks like we could hold him on assault and battery if you testify against him. I doubt we can make arson charges stick. He'll likely make bail in a few days unless we have something more we can come up with. Anything to add to my report?"

"No."

Gregg shook his head. "You need to testify, Beaumont. The man's in league with the devil."

"No. I won't, Fischer. Nothing you can say will make me change my mind."

Beaumont probably hoped the sinner might repent. Gregg didn't hold out any hope in that regard. He faced Skylar. "I'll give a statement. Gladly."

"Come by my office in the morning."

"On one condition."

"Yeah?"

"Where's Joanna Beaumont."

Aubrey wheeled toward Gregg. "What do you mean, Fischer? She's dead."

"No. She's not." He faced Skylar. "Is she?"

Skylar still refused to confess.

"I'll bet my last dollar she's in witness protection."

Skylar glanced toward the building debris. "I don't know what you're talking about."

Beaumont gripped Skylar's shoulders. "Lucas, where's my wife."

Skylar glared as he pushed Beaumont's hands from his torso. "Fine. Just remember, Fischer, to show up tomorrow morning with your testimony. You're partially right. Joanna is alive, and she was under my protection."

Beaumont paled. "Was? What does that mean. Where is she now?"

Skylar sighed. "She refused further protection. Her right."

"You let her go? In her condition?"

"My plan was to put both her and Juarez under arrest."

"That's a plan?"

"Best option I have. She'd have been better off in prison than on the street. Officer Casey followed her, and she unwittingly led us to Juarez's headquarters. We sent backup and searched the building. Got Juarez, but there was no sign of Joanna. We're doing a sweep of the vicinity."

Beaumont scowled. "Fischer, I have to find her."

"We will buddy. I'll help."

Skylar's cell buzzed, and he glanced at his phone. "You two don't go anywhere. I have to take this call, then I'll be right back. Let the police do their job. Makes no sense for them to search for you as well."

As Skylar stepped to the side, Beaumont grit his teeth and glared. "You knew she was alive and didn't tell me?"

"I only figured things out late this afternoon. I didn't have a chance to say anything until now, did I?"

Beaumont growled. "I guess not."

Skylar returned. "The police found Joanna unconscious on the pavement near Juarez headquarters. An ambulance has taken her to Community Hospital."

CHAPTER 31

Aubrey checked his watch. Five minutes wasted while he stood in the cafeteria line. His head still ached, a reminder of last night's horror—the whole scene at Redemption's Corner blurred, like looking through cracked glass.

Other than Joanna had been found, he knew nothing of her condition. Since Fischer had no vehicle handy, Aubrey had to scramble to find a ride to the hospital, not knowing if Joanna were alive or dead. Seemed everyone had other agendas than the welfare of a drug addict in the last throes of a horrible illness. Dozens of people focused on police reports and clean up. Thankfully, the mission paperwork had been filed in a fireproof safe. The work would survive.

He'd reached Cynthia, who rushed to his aid, though she had to pack for her return to Chicago. He wished she'd stay to help with rebuilding Redemption's Corner. He supposed he understood why she wanted to leave.

Fischer had been a fool. Why couldn't he accept Cynthia loved him in a way she could never love a minister tied to a passion that consumed him?

Thuds, clangs, and shouts competed for his attention. He barely heard his phone chime. He thought he'd muted the thing. If one considered the events of yesterday, he had a right to be a bit distracted.

He glanced at the caller ID. Fischer. Aubrey shook his head. Perhaps he'd forgive the fool someday. After all, Fischer did risk his life in a misguided attempt to save a friend. But forgiveness would have to wait. Right now, Aubrey's only concern was for Joanna.

He answered his cell with his officious voice. "Beaumont here."

"Where are you?"

"Where do you think? I'm at the hospital."

The cashier shot him a poisonous glare. "That's five dollars and thirty-five cents."

"Look, I'll call you right back."

He paid for his coffee and donut, took the elevator to the lobby and went outside. The crisp winter air felt as cold as his feelings toward Fischer. Aubrey's head said he shouldn't put the whole blame on his former friend, though. The man had done what he thought best, albeit lucrative. Aubrey pulled out his phone. Should he return the call now?

Perhaps confusion was more to blame for Aubrey's numb spirit than his bitterness toward Fischer. The question Aubrey could not answer. Why had God brought Joanna to him after all this time only to take her away? He leaned against a column and punched Fischer's number.

He blurted his concern before any exchange of pleasantries. "I thought maybe you cut me off, so you didn't have to talk to me."

"Wasn't the best place to hold a conversation."

"How's Joanna?"

"Do you care?"

"Yes, I do."

"No change. She's still unconscious. I came down to the cafeteria to get a cup of coffee and then make calls. Congressman and Mrs. Curtis expect to visit this morning, perhaps hold a news conference. They're going public with Joanna's story."

"Really? Everything?"

"Everything. They hope full disclosure will bring support for Redemption's Corner. We're going to find another home. Hopefully, not far from where we were."

"How did the kids take the news?"

Another unanswered question … why a God of mercy had not allowed Joanna to see her children. Sometimes he struggled to worship a God of enigma. Yet, like Job, he knew he had no other hope. "Not well, at first."

"Have they come to visit?"

"Paul stayed outside Joanna's room and waved for me to come out. He cried for his mother like a baby, but refused to go in. Bradley plans to bring Trish with him if Joanna regains consciousness."

"And Darlene?"

"She's angry, confused."

"She's a good kid. She'll come around."

Aubrey chewed his lower lip. Not without a Holy Ghost intervention. "The doctor says Joanna is very near the end and may not regain consciousness. I'm afraid a reconciliation with the children will not happen this side of heaven."

"Remember the sermon you preached on God's ability to reach beyond our circumstances?"

"Yeah." Funny that Fischer would recall any sermons, especially those he characterized as a good nap time. Aubrey shook his head with the thought. What few sermons of his Fischer had attended, he seemed to sleep through. Never underestimate the power of the Holy Spirit to penetrate through the groggiest of minds.

"Do you remember the verse you quoted?"

"From Numbers. Is the arm of the Lord short?"

"You said so yourself. God doesn't always answer our prayers in the way we think he should. Yet, he always answers for the best, regardless of our selfish petitions."

"She prayed for purpose, Fischer. Why didn't God give her that?"

"He has. You're too deep in grief to see his purpose in all that has happened. Now, what's the rest of the verse?"

"Stand back and see what the Lord will do."

"Exactly."

Aubrey's sigh emerged from his deep well of doubt. "Maybe you should be a minister. Good counsel. Thanks, Fischer."

"I'll leave the preaching to you, Beaumont." Fischer's cough meant he would advance to the real purpose of his call. "Any word from Cynthia? I've tried her cell several times. Percy's phone's been disconnected."

"You didn't know?"

"Know what?"

"Percy went to the nursing home yesterday. Cynthia's flight leaves in a few hours."

"Flight? Where?"

"She's decided to return to Chicago."

"Where's she flying out of?"

"BWI." Silence. "Fischer? You there?" Aubrey smiled as he disconnected. *Lord, I hope he catches her.*

A commotion accompanied the surprise greeting. "Hello, Aubrey."

He turned toward the older woman's voice. "Mrs. Curtis. I didn't expect you until later."

The congressman stepped from the limo and joined his wife. A dozen or so reporters swarmed around them and cast questions like a horde of fishermen. He pulled Aubrey to the side. "Forget the hounds for the moment. How's our Joanna?"

"Still unconscious. No change since you left last night."

Mrs. Curtis squeezed Aubrey's hand. "We're so sorry. None of us wanted this outcome. We all hoped to have her a little longer. May we see her now? Maybe the Lord will let her know on some level that we're there."

"I'll give you a few moments alone with her before I come up."

Congressman Curtis shook Aubrey's hand. "You're truly a man after God's heart, Aubrey. I'm proud to have you as a son-in-law." Sadness pulled at Mrs. Curtis's attempted smile as she leaned against her husband for support. Washington's elite strode hand in hand as they encountered their most personal grief.

Gregg parked his car in the first available space in the short-term parking lot. He tried Cynthia's cell one more time. "C'mon, answer." He'd left the same voice mail at least a dozen times in the space of thirty minutes. "Cynthia. I'm so sorry. Please, stay."

He'd hung up on Beaumont before he found out which flight. He checked the departure schedules. She could be on one of three different departures. How could he know which? Southwest would be leaving within the hour and was most likely the one Cynthia would have booked. He checked the gate number ... at the other end of the airport.

What excuse could he give to get through security?

Maybe if he bought a ticket. Still enough time. He put on his best casual walk as he sauntered up to the ticket counter. A youngish blonde woman fiddled with paperwork. She must have sensed a presence though she never looked up. "May I help you?"

"Just received word my mother's in bad shape." He placed one arm on the counter and leaned in. He forced his voice at least two octaves lower. "Please tell me you have a seat on this flight to Chicago?"

"Let me check, sir."

Sir? He'd never felt so insulted by a polite address. Granted, he'd gained a few pounds since college days. Yet, once upon a time he could charm a young girl with a smile. Maybe with his slight paunch and a receding hairline, seduction no longer worked.

Icy blue eyes stared back. "This flight is full, sir. I can book you on the 4:30 this afternoon?" She glanced over the counter. "Would give you time to go home and pack a suitcase."

When charm failed, money often talked. He pulled out a hundred-dollar bill. "Are you absolutely sure? Could you check again, please?"

She took the bribe, and expertly slipped the cash under her sleeve. "I'll see what I can do." She clicked and clacked for an interminable five minutes. "You're in luck. I see there's been a recent cancellation."

Cancelled or bumped? Didn't matter. He'd managed to get a seat.

She leaned forward with a provocative toss of her golden curls. "May I have your name?"

"Greggory Fischer."

More clicks and clacks. "I need two forms of identification, Mr. Fischer."

He showed her his driver's license and passport.

When he looked up, two armed guards stood on either side. The older of the two scowled. "Come with us, sir."

Great. Was he branded a suspected terrorist? As the men led him toward a private cubicle, the blonde clerk took out Gregg's bribe money from her sleeve. "Here's the evidence."

The guards escorted him from the service desk toward a curtained area. "Wait here."

Within a few minutes, a suited man entered the cubicle. "ID?"

"I just showed the girl." Gregg squinted to read the man's tag. Tad Sherman, Security Chief. "Why call in the bigwigs. This is all a misunderstanding. I'm not a terrorist."

"Perhaps not. Still, you bribed an airport official. You seem pretty determined to get on that particular flight."

Gregg found himself at the opposite end of an interrogation. The whole scene might be amusing, except now he'd miss Cynthia's flight. "Can't we forget about this? Honest. I know I shouldn't have tried to bribe the young lady. I only wanted to see my girlfriend before her plane leaves."

The younger guard leaned forward. "Why? Need to give her something? Like a bomb, maybe?"

Paranoia ran rampant. Reason would not work. Gregg leaned back against the chair. "Doesn't matter now, anyway. I'll never reach the gate in time." He pulled out his PI license. "Here. Add this to your list of identifiers."

Security Chief Sherman examined Gregg's credentials. "I'll need to verify your story. Wait here."

Gregg ping-ponged glances from one guard to the other. Should he try to make conversation? Why not? "So … worked at this job long?"

166

Silence. Not even a smile.

He stared ahead. Best not to rile either one further—they might slap handcuffs on him.

After ten long minutes, Chief Sherman returned. "Seems you have friends in high places."

"I do?"

"Your employer referred us to Congressman Curtis's office. They vouched for you. Although, you will receive a citation and a fine."

"Not going to jail?"

"Not this time. As I'd say to my son, 'I hope you learned your lesson, young man.'"

"Very funny. Am I free to leave?"

"Not to Chicago. As a precaution, we'll escort you to your vehicle."

Gregg piled into the front seat and started the motor while Frick and Frack stood off to the side as if waiting for him to pull out. One of them wrote something on a pad. His license number?

He sighed from defeat. He'd failed at the one romantic thing he'd ever tried to do. He could only hope Cynthia would call when she reached Chicago.

What if she didn't?

He brightened with the thought. He'd found her once. He'd find her again. He'd fly out there and convince her to return. Or … why not live in Chicago? Briggs had an office there. He could ask for a transfer. It's not like he had anything here in DC to hold him. Not even a best friend.

He pulled onto the Interstate when his cell buzzed with a missed message notice. Law or no law, he checked the text from Cynthia. *I canceled my flight. Meet me at Dad's.*

CHAPTER 32

Joanna moaned as she forced her eyes open. "Aubrey? Where ... where am I?" She stretched. Am I still alive? She touched her face, the oxygen mask heavy against her sensitive skin.

Her eyes focused on Aubrey who sat next to her bed. "Where am I?"

"You're at Community Hospital. The ambulance brought you here late Sunday night. You've been unconscious since then." He lifted the stray strains of hair caught underneath the mask. She pleasured in the warmth of his touch.

The peaceful moment passed as she gasped for air, as if under water, unable to breathe. She forced another unimportant question. "What time is it?"

"Almost eleven. Hush, Joanna, save your strength. You don't have to say anything. It must be painful for you to talk."

Was she here in this world or in the next. The sense of floating, and yet, she could feel Aubrey's hands. No words could come. She tried to smile. Did she succeed? Aubrey's mist-filled eyes indicated perhaps she had.

He lay on the bed next to her and cradled her head on his shoulder. "Pain?"

She shook her head. Oddly, not much. More like a numbness. She closed her eyes.

Hours could have passed as he held her while she drifted in and out.

Lord, help me speak the words Aubrey needs to hear. She fumbled at her oxygen mask. When Aubrey lifted the barrier, she breathed with resolve. "I remember Stowe."

He kissed her hand. "I'll always remember the moment I first saw you. You sat alone and sipped cinnamon tea. You seemed out of place and yet not so out of place at the same time. I knew I'd ask you to marry me before I crossed the room to introduce myself."

The memory chased the cold, her blanket of imminent transport. She forced the words with her next breath. "Spread my ashes there."

"I promise. Now rest, darling."

She nestled tighter against Aubrey's shoulder. He kissed her cheek. If only she could pass now. What kept her alive? Did Aubrey's love keep her here? She glanced toward her table. "I'd like cinnamon tea."

He hesitated before he rose. Did he know she would be gone when he returned?

"I'll get you a cup. Your parents are here. They've visited a few times. Now that you're awake, would you like to see them?"

She nodded.

Her eyes closed as Aubrey left the room. She'd heard death was akin to a fall. What did the living know about dying? She hovered between here and eternity, the sensation more disorienting than peaceful. What held her to this world? Aubrey was safe, and he'd forgiven her. She knew the children would also forgive her in time. Yet she still could not surrender.

She willed her eyes open. An elderly couple stood by her bed. She barely recognized them. The woman laid a cold compress across Joanna's forehead, the same woman who'd comforted her countless times in her youth. Joanna welcomed her mother's love.

A male voice carried on the air. "You're awake? Good."

"Daddy?"

He grasped her hand. As he talked, his words seemed jumbled, yet Joanna could understand his intention. Peace finally came with her earthly father's forgiveness.

Mother had moved to the other side of the bed. She held Joanna's hand. "Go to Jesus, child." A familiar lullaby filled the room, the one Mother used to sing to a frightened little Joanna when the night brought imagined monsters.

Light descended. "Home!"

CHAPTER 33

Aubrey pecked his new daughter-in-law on the cheek. "Welcome to the family, Trish. If my son doesn't treat you right, you tell me. I'll spank him."

Bradley leaned in toward his bride. "He's not kidding, you know."

If only Joanna could have lived to see her Bradley wed. The boys finally came to terms with Joanna's life and death. Lacking the balm faith offers, Darlene required more time.

She will come around. Trust me.

I will, Lord.

At least she'd come to the wedding and sat with the congressman and his wife. Perhaps her grandparents would help her find the courage to forgive.

Aubrey shook Congressman Curtis's hand. "Merry Christmas. I'm glad you're here."

"Merry Christmas to you too." Congressman Curtis leaned toward Darlene. "Would you do an old man the honor of a dance?"

She surrendered a glimmer of a smile.

Mrs. Curtis wiped her eyes with an embroidered handkerchief. "We owe you a great deal, Aubrey. You brought Joanna and her children back to us."

The bandleader tapped the mic for attention. "This next song is dedicated to the bride by his adoring groom. Let's have Bradley and Trish up on the dance floor."

To the melody of "You Raise Me Up," Bradley and Trish snuggled together, soon joined by others including Darlene and Congressman Curtis.

Aubrey's thoughts wandered to Stowe Mountain, the pinnacle of Joanna's love. Remorse left a soul drained. Yet, he could not help but wonder what life with Joanna might have been if not for the drugs. How happy they'd been during her stints of sobriety. What man's invention tried to tear apart, in the end, love survived … God's love.

She'd prayed for her life to have a purpose. Perhaps the Lord showed her this scene from a heavenly seat. "You did this, Joanna," he whispered. "Your children know their heritage and how much you loved them even through the worst of your addiction."

If not for Joanna, Redemption's Corner would not have been birthed.

Aubrey turned as if he sensed her presence. Perhaps in some way he did.

He wandered to Fischer and Cynthia's table. "Merry Christmas, you two."

"Merry Christmas, Aubrey."

He accepted Fischer's manly hug. "Merry Christmas, buddy. Great wedding."

"Glad you're here."

Fischer returned to his seat and held Cynthia's hand. They gazed at one another like love-struck teenagers.

"So?"

"We'll be fine. She knows I'm an idiot but loves me anyway."

Pressed with a need for fresh air, Aubrey stepped outside. The weather was unusually warm for December. He took the moment to plan the next few days and his trip to Stowe where he'd arranged for a private memorial in Joanna's honor.

He'd spent a decade and a half in search of her after she left him for good. He'd imagined himself like Hosea of old, a man bound by a promise. He'd lived so much in the past, he could not imagine a future. There was Redemption's Corner, at the very least. Then what? He supposed God had more mountains for him to climb and deserts for him to cross, especially with Juarez out on bail.

This much he knew—though the where might be a mystery—God had already paved the way.

ABOUT THE AUTHOR

God is able to turn our worst past into our best future. This is the theme of every Rondeau book. A veteran social worker, Rondeau delves into the intricacies of human relationships, earning her critical acclaim for her heart-warming stories of deliverance and forgiveness. The author now resides in Hagerstown, MD with her best friend in life, her husband of forty years. Active in her local church, she enjoys playing the occasional round of golf, a common feature in many of her books. Readers may contact the author through Facebook, Twitter, Goodreads, Google Plus, Pinterest, and Instagram or visit her website: www.lindarondeau.com.